I'M GONNA BURY YOU!

BY GENE NEILL

Foreword by

MERLIN CAROTHERS

Publisher

THE VOICE OF TRIUMPH, INC

P. O. Box 78

Mayo, Florida 32066

Copyright

The Voice of Triumph, Inc.

P. O. Box 78

Mayo, Florida 32066

I'M GONNA'BURY YOU!

SEVENTEENTH PRINTING

Published by

The Voice of Triumph, Inc.,

ISBN 0-9608028-0-0

THIS BOOK IS DEDICATED TO THE MANY
PEOPLE WHOSE LOVE, SUPPORT AND
PRAYERS MADE IT POSSIBLE!

THANK YOU ONE AND ALL.

PREFACE

Every word of this incredible story is true.

And it all happened just like it says here in these pages. As unbelievable as it may sound.

The moral and ethical degeneracy and decay of our government and of our world is deeper and more cancerous than most comprehend. And it lurks just beyond the shadows in every police station and courthouse and capitol of the world.

Yet as low as I sank at one time — and horrible as the crimes were which I committed — and as filled with violence and corruption and vice and greed as our government is — I want to tell you something!

We've got to have order.

We've got to have police. And jails. And prisons. Otherwise we have only chaos!

And we must live together in a structured society. Obeying the laws and the police. And having care and love for one another.

Only those who do shall survive.

-Gene Neill

FOREWORD

When you meet some men, you know they are for real. Nothing phony. No gimmicks. Nothing to push. But Jesus. This is Gene Neill. A man's man. Solid. Yet sensitive and filled with love for everyone.

Reading this book will be one of the most unique experiences of your life. It is exciting and romantic and yet reaches into a depth of suffering few have experienced. When you have finished these pages you will long to meet Gene Neill. If you do meet him, you will be thrilled to see a man who loves God with every part of his being.

But a far more important event will take place as you read Gene's story. Your faith will be lifted to a new height. Regardless of how weak or strong your faith is, when you complete the book you will rejoice and shout within, *"Now I believe in Jesus more than ever!"* Gene's remarkable, amazing, exciting experience in prison will fill you with an explosion of praise that will probably stay with you forever. Everything that you have and enjoy will be twice as important to you when you have read the final page of *"I'm Gonna' Bury You!"*

-Merlin R. Carothers

1   "YOU'RE NEVER GOIN' HOME!"

"You're never going home, big shot!" The huge guard laughed as he unshackled the chains from my waist and arms. *"So enjoy your stay!"*

But before we walked down the ramp into the gloom of the stone tunnel, I stretched from the cramped fatigue of the long ride in chains and looked up once more at the sky. One last look at the world. But it was cold and grey and foreboding, and everything was winter dead. The grass and the trees and the world.

And me.

And as the four of us moved on down into the ground, I could feel the dampness and cold in my bare·feet, and smell the rancid slime on the tunnel walls. A putrid smell which was to be my ceaseless companion for a long time. And I shuddered as the massive steel doors boomed together behind us. But we kept walking on and on into the depths, to the cadence of the steel-tipped boots of the big men at my side.

Then I heard a man scream.

And then more steel slamming against steel. And men sobbing and groaning and crying. Agonizing sounds which never stilled. But the others with me didn't even notice.

"You can't have a toothbrush or soap or razor." One of them warned. "'Cause you can kill yourself or one of us with any of them things. And no mail for now, and you can't see the chaplain or the doctor, or leave your cell for *nothin'*. Once a week we'll come down and get you and put you in a shower where you can wash off with sand soap. And when we put your food on the floor outside your door, you stand way back in your cell while we open the door. Then get down on the floor and reach out real slow with one hand and drag the tray into your cell. But don't let any part of you but your hand come out the door or we'll stomp you. And there'll always be at least three of us there to do the job!"

"Yeah, but you're gonna be in real good company, Mr. Big-Shot Prosecutor!" One of the others laughed. "'Cause the cannibal's gonna be right across from you. He's the one they caught when the cop saw him walkin' down the street with a man's hand hangin' out of his pocket! He'd just killed an old wino and eaten his heart while it was still beatin'. Just for kicks. And he was jus' takin' a little snack home for dinner! Ha!"

"And the guy on the other side of you has been in for sixty-four years." The third guard bragged. "Old Chief we call him. An Indian. Robbed a stage coach and killed the driver back in Oklahoma Territory. And is he ever doin' bad time! Hates every miserable minute of it."

But we just kept walking on, perhaps a quarter of a mile, until we reached a small steel door with a slit in the front. One of them unlocked it with a massive bronze key, threw my greasy old blanket and pillow in onto the caked floor and shoved me into the suffocating darkness inside.

"Get in, big shot!" He snarled. "We'll be back for you in fifty years!"

And he wasn't smiling.

I had been sentenced by Judge C. Clyde Atkins, a Federal District Court Judge in Miami, Florida, to serve fifty years, and I still had a dozen federal indictments pending which carried another possible one hundred and twenty years. And here I was, in the "hole." Solitary confinement. In one of the most maximum security federal prisons in the nation in Springfield, Missouri. Where they kept cannibals and stagecoach robbers and where the "bird-man of Alcatraz" died all alone. An empty old man.

"Fifty years!" My heart pounded as I glanced numbly around at my new home. "So this is it! So this is my home for the rest of my life. So this is where I'm going to die someday. I wonder how long it will take."

And it was horrible and hideous and indescribable. There was no air and the stench was loathsome and the sweat dripped off me onto the stone floor as I reached out with my arms to measure the distance between the stone walls.

"I can touch from wall to wall this way, and almost from wall to wall that way." I noticed. *"My God why does it have to be so small!"* Must

3

be about six by nine. And just a steel slab with a slimy little two-inch rubber pad for a mattress. And a foul smelling little brown toilet. And a filthy little sink. And stains and matter of all kind dripping from the walls and ceiling!"

"Can I possibly sleep over here?" I remember hoping. "Near the outside edge of the bunk so I don't rub against that human stuff smeared on the wall? But then the bunk is just as bad. So I guess it won't matter. And I might as well get used to it!"

And the heat was overpowering and unbearable as it came boiling out of a steel register over the toilet. I tried pressing my face against the filthy steel door for coolness, but even it was warm and repelling. And as I gasped to breathe I tore my dripping clothes off and stood there naked and sweating and my heart pounding.

And then I saw the writing on the walls. Incredible words of perverted old men whose very souls were already in the flaming pit of eternal hell. Not the flippant or dirty or erotic scatological and sexual graffiti of bus station toilets, but the depraved and morose ramblings and scribbling of deranged and morbid and screaming animals.

And oh so pitiable!

Particularly the dates. And months. And years. Little areas on the walls where broken old men had started checking off each day of their unbearable lives as endless time there in that horrible tomb stood still for them. Broken old men like me. There would be the date they first came into the cell. And then the date of the next day and the next and the next. And then you could see where they had

4

lost count of the date and had to just start making marks to keep track. Mark after mark after mark. On and on and on through years and years and years of endless agony and 'horror and sobbing and despair. Always alone. Broken and lonely and dying. *Screaming lonely!* And then the marks would get weaker and weaker. And then finally just trail off.

Trail off into an unmarked prison grave.

Or an insane asylum.

Alone. All alone.

And there was a tiny ray of sunshine which beamed in hauntingly against the wall over my bunk from a high, tiny barred opening which led out into a barren and enclosed courtyard beyond. And the little spot of light traced a tiny arc across my wall for only a few moments each day as the sun headed down toward the night. And then it was gone. A fleeting little will-o'-the-wisp. Now here. Now gone.

But as the mighty sun of our majestic solar system crept its way ever so slowly and imperceptibly southward toward the winter solstice, some poor and now long-dead soul had noticed after many months how the tiny arc of light had crept gradually higher and higher up the slimy wall. And with his wretched and trembling old hand he had begun tracing the arc each month as it moved upward and upward. Month after month until December of that year.

Many years ago.

And then he had traced the tiny little arc downward with forlorn and depraved regularity as the sun crawled ever so slowly back up toward the summer solstice that year. Until June.

And then back up another year. And then back down.

And then back up another year. And then back down.

Month after endless month. Year after desolate year. On and on into death's oblivion.

"Oh my God such horror!" I exclaimed out loud! "A second is a lifetime. An hour is indescribable. A day is unbearable and unthinkable here in this sweltering and vile madness!"

"And fifty years the judge said! Fifty years in this loathsome, horrible little solitary cell. Alone. And naked and sweating. Waiting for an endless lifetime to drag slowly by in tears. Waiting for death to comfort me!"

And as the staggering and ghastly and hideous reality of that endless living death crushed down on me like a mountain crushing down on a coal miner deep within the black bowels of the earth, I threw myself to the slimy floor and sobbed and sobbed. And as I writhed naked there in that desolate horror, my entire life passed in array before me. A bizarre and fantastic tableau. An incredible lifetime of frantic yet fruitless search for reality.

2   NOBODY EVER SAID ANYTHING ABOUT JESUS

And the first thing I thought about was my old great granddad.

We don't know a whole lot about old great granddad James Gilflllen except that he loved the Lord Jesus! Because shortly after he came over at age sixteen from the highlands of parish Cumberwarthen, Scotland, in 1828, he started preaching. Tramping up and down all over the mountains of Pennsylvania and Ohio preaching in the Erie Conference of the Methodist Church. But you can also read of his love for the Lord in the mute witness of the 122 year old marginal notes in the big old pulpit Bible he lugged all over those rugged slopes.

A man of God.

But as his children and grandchildren began to prosper there in Pennsylvania and West Virginia they seemed to drift further and further from the foot of the Cross. Funny how prosperity does that sometimes.

And I suppose my poor old father was about as far from the Lord as anyone can get. Yet he was right slap-dab in the middle of religion. A very outspoken and very proudly self-made dentist of considerable wealth, he never missed a Methodist service. He sang in the choir and taught Sunday School and never loved anybody. Least of all himself. He was always extraordinarily aggressive, intolerant, bigoted and brilliant. Miserly and miserable.

And when I was born in Fairmont, West Virginia, in 1931, we had a huge house in the best section of town and a big summer camp out in the mountains by the Tygart's Valley River and a big Lincoln automobile and all kinds of worldly things.

But there was never much joy around our house. And not much love.

Oh, as a little lad I used to love to explore the woods out there around the camp or pad barefooted through the summer shade down the cool clay road by the river. Mother would give me a nickel and I would run all the way down that old road and across the bridge a couple of miles to the little general store in Colfax where I would buy a big piece of candy or a soda. And it was as much fun as a circus!

And when we used to go out in the country to old granddad Eldora Moran's farm in Catawba for the weekend, it was just the greatest thing in the whole wide world! Because there were cows and horses and chickens and dogs to play with. And haymows and barns. And the outhouse and the bats in the attic and grandma's applesauce pies. And the old pump organ. He was my mother's father, and old

8

granddad Eldora Moran had more love than any man who ever lived. And I could feel it. Everybody could.

And then there were the yearly Morgan reunions up on the hill from his farm in the shade of the ageless Sycamores by the little old frame Mount Zion Church. Mount Zion Church — topped off by the big old oak weathervane granddad Moran had hand-carved in the shape of a fist with the index finger pointing triumphantly and eternally heavenward! A *"One Way"* sign even way back in those mountains a hundred years ago. And boy, there was all day eatin' and all day preachin' and all day singin' at those get togethers! And they were even *better* than a circus!

And of course in the winter time there was snow sledding and Christmas days and new tricycles and all those things that will keep a little boy smiling.

But I don't remember anybody ever talking about a real living Jesus. Oh I remember them telling me at Christmas and Easter time about some man who lived a couple of thousand years ago who was a real good man. But nobody ever said anything about a real living Jesus.

And when I was seven my mother, father, brother and I moved from West Virginia down to wealthy Coral Gables, Florida. The fancy suburb of Miami. And our big new marble-floored mansion was right across the street from the huge rich Coral Gables First Methodist Church.

And I can still remember my first Sunday School lessons:

"You cannot *really* believe the Bible you know." The little lady teacher with the big diamond ring used to warn us. "Because it does not really mean what it says. It is just a nice storybook to tell you that if you live good lives and obey your mommies and daddies you will all go to heaven one day. *Now won't that be nice?*"

"Yes Miz Banky." We all dutifully intoned.

"And as for that story about Noah and the flood," she continued, "it of course did not happen that way either. The world could not have been covered with water. That is just another story to show you that if you are bad God is going to punish you. And of course Peter *did not really* walk on the water because that is not possible either. We all know that. That is just another little story too."

"Yes MizBanky."

"Boy, what a silly waste of time this old place is!" My busy little mind rebelled. *"I could be ridin' my bike or climin' trees or anything!"*

And I was right. I might as well have been. Yet I kept on going there dutifully every Sunday, year in and year out. First because my folks made me. Then just because it seemed like the thing to do.

After all, everybody else was doing it.

And what a church it was! The biggest and richest and fanciest church in all Miami. Worth millions of dollars. And as a tiny lad listening to grown-up talk I can remember all the scandals and gossips and back-biting. And I remember all the Cadillac's and cigarettes and furs and diamonds and drinking and how the preachers were always getting fired if they said the wrong things. And how everybody was always talking about money and salaries and contributions and tax deductions.

But nobody ever talked about Jesus.

And I remember my dad and all the other folks in the church were sick all the time and filled with worries and anxieties and troubles. Always. But nobody ever said anything about a God who could do something about all that. But then, come to think of it, I don't remember anybody ever saying anything about praying for that matter.

And I know nobody ever mentioned Jesus.

Oh there were always lots of things going on in the church. There were committees and finance campaigns and circles and expansion programs and drives and choirs and meetings. And there were all kinds of parties and picnics and covered-dish suppers and on and on.

But nobody ever talked about Jesus.

There were huge stained glass windows and velvet draperies everywhere, and massive mahogany altars and pulpits and railings and pews and mammoth hand-carved doors. And *real* gold candlesticks and crosses and collection plates. If you donated enough money you could have a gold plaque put up with your name on it so everybody could see it. There were lots of satin robes and gowns. Even the old janitor used to wear a satin robe on Sundays.

But nobody ever talked about Jesus.

And it bothered me. In fact life in general bothered me. And I seemed to always be looking for something more in life than what I could see with my eyes. Something always seemed to be missing! Something invisible and illusive and just right around the next corner. Or just over the next hill. Or in the next country.

Yet I felt like I was the only person in the whole world who even noticed it was missing. *And it was something you just could not live without!* And yet nobody else seemed to understand at all. Nobody else even seemed to notice it was missing. Or care.

And I could not understand why they couldn't see it was missing! Why couldn't they see there was something missing in life!

And I used to cry a lot. All alone.

And my wonderful and love-filled mother would come in and try to sooth me as I lay there on my bed sobbing.

"Gene, what's wrong dear?" Her voice would tremble.

"I don't know Mamma. I don't know! I'm just unhappy. And that's all I know. **I just don't know!**" And that was all I knew to say.

But I remember my brother Jim never cried. He never even noticed that something was missing. Always self-sufficient and well organized. And satisfied.

And later in life as I was to search more and more desperately, he was to tell me over and over again that I was just running away from

12

myself. And that I would have to settle down and stop all this nonsense.

He never understood either.

So one Sunday when I was a junior in high school I urged my pal George Champion, "Hey, let's skip church this Sunday and spend the day out in the glades snake hunting.'

"Good idea!" He agreed, and off we went in my Model "A". We had been snake and orchid hunting off and on for a year or so together, and used to sell the live water moccasins and rattlers to the snake farms, more for fun than for the money. In fact I frequently had a dozen or so big poisonous water moccasins and rattlesnakes in big open-top cardboard boxes out in our garage where our sweet old black maid Idella had to do the ironing.

"Lawd! Have mussy!" She used to plead with me, smiling just a tiny bit. "When you gonna' git dem tings *out o' dis place!?"*

And we got pretty good at the lore of the Everglades as we journeyed deeper and deeper into the trackless and ageless swamps.

Glades buggies were unheard of in those days, and only a few of the Seminole Indians along the Tamiami Trail had old wooden air boats with Ford V-8 60's in them. And they only used them for frogging right there along the highway.

But we plunged on into the unknown. Deeper and deeper into the cool dark cypress cathedrals where the primeval silence was only

13

broken by deer and otter and wild turkeys. Where incredibly hued and delicately formed orchids gracefully waved from every mossy bough. Where the stillness was majestic and powerful and eternal. And where the sweet smells of wild flowers and bubbling streams and moss mingled and lured us tantalizingly deeper into the beyond.

And something there touched me.

Or Someone.

For I began to feel for the first time in my life that there was meaning and warmth and beauty and an eternal quality to life which lay somehow right there where I was standing. Or maybe just beyond the next hammock. *It was right there and I could almost touch and feel it!* Almost. Not quite. And George felt it too and was moved by it and so we came back every weekend, again and again for a year. Going deeper each time.

"Listen George!" I used to say as we would stand in awe as the soft summer wind whispered his secrets to the saw grass and to the tall slash pines. And we would sit for hours in the ageless oak forest chapels watching the tiny otters gleefully sliding down the upturned roots of an old hurricane-felled cypress. And the squirrels would romp and play and the majestic white ibis would feed nearby as a noble big buck nibbled at the new green leaflets across the crystal pond.

I was a little boy playing under the very Throne of Almighty God, and never knew it. I could sense His footprints there all around me. But I didn't know to look up. Nobody had ever told me to. Nobody ever told me there would be anyone there even if I **did** look up.

And a great yearning and longing began to gnaw a hole into my heart. A big God-shaped hole which was going to get bigger and bigger as the years drew on and on. A big God-shaped hole which I was destined to travel to the very ends of this planet to try to fill. *Which I was destined to sink to the lowest depths of depravity and degeneracy to try to fill.* A big God-shaped hole which will destroy a man if it is not filled in time.

And there's so little time.

But then after high school when my ambitious father insisted that I become a wealthy dentist like he, I was shipped off to Emory University in Atlanta, Georgia, to pursue that grand profession. And the infinite peace and stillness and ageless strength of my cypress cathedrals were all gone now. I had wanted to be a forest ranger so I could stay there forever, but Dad said that was juvenile and beneath my intelligence.

So there I was in big old dirty Atlanta. With fraternities and sororities and beer and cigarettes and girls and all those other things you think you've got to do if you want to belong. All those things with which everybody else is secretly trying so desperately to fill his own God-shaped hole. And with which I was to try so frantically to fill mine.

"All the *really big men* on campus are Sigma Chi's." The sophisticated senior in the neat cashmere sweater and new white bucks confided at the rush party. "And if you're really going to be on the *inside* here at Emory this is the fraternity for you. And we have some really out-of-sight parties and all the little chicks from Agnes Scott come over and really groove on us and we really live it up. And we're the biggest and the oldest and the best."

And as he went on and on my young mind flashed back longingly from all that razzle dazzle to the peaceful shade and serene silence of my ageless oak and moss cathedrals. And to that loving fullness and incredible peace I had known there in my secret hiding place. That fullness which was never to be recaptured for a million miles and a million years.

But then there was that terrible gnawing hole again, and I knew I had to fill it with something!

"O.K. Fine! Where do I sign up?" I gave in as he lit my cigarette and handed me my first cold Champale. And "*Shazam*!" Little Captain Marvel was now suddenly the big man on campus! A B.M.O.C. with all the groovy clothes and just the right kind of mixed drink and the right kind of imported beers and the English Oval Cigarettes and the hopped-up car and the little black book full of willing phone numbers. Empty little phone numbers who secretly were searching just as desperately and just as fruitlessly as the big man on campus.

And one of them was a rich little high school senior named Beverly. Beautiful, poised, stagy and empty. A blind date to an exclusive little cocktail dance. And after that and a few more whirlwind courtings the big hollow man swept the hollow little girl off her feet by pinning her with his flashy jeweled Sigma Chi pin — a mating that was to end in terrible tragedy eleven years later.

16

But as the little blond and her sophisticated big college man raced around Atlanta for a year of petting and partying, his grades fell from bad to worse until one day the dean frowned, "Gene, I'm not expelling you but there's something missing in your life. And until you find it and get hold of yourself you're just not going to be able to make it here. Or anywhere. So don't come back next quarter. *Go find yourself! And settle down!*"

"Oh my God!" I thought. "Doesn't he know how terribly desperately *I want to find myself!* Doesn't he know how tragically *I am* searching for something real in life to cling to! Oh how I wish I could cry out to him! Or to someone! Or to die!"

And my heart lunged out for my secret cathedrals back in the prehistoric everglade jungles. But they were gone. Forever.

But since my father had never known failure, he never understood my despair. And since he had never cried, he never understood my tears. He used to boast, when he saw me crying, that he had never cried in his life. And so when I transferred to the University of Miami in the summer of 1950 he only made my emptiness greater by his relentless reproach and derision.

But he never said anything about Jesus.

Yet within the pool of my mother's beautiful brown eyes I could always sense an eternal quality of peace and love which reminded me of what I saw in that bottomless pool in the timeless cathedral with the orchids and otters and moss.

17

And I did fairly well scholastically for the first quarter, but then Beverly came down from Atlanta and matriculated in the fall and we began roaring around in fraternity life all over again. And I bought a real slick '39 Ford coupe with sixteen coats of black lacquer and a big engine and a set of pipes that just wouldn't quit. And all of a sudden I was the big man on campus again. Trying to fill that hole. But only making it bigger every day.

And I would cry myself to sleep at nights not even knowing why I was crying. Just like when I was a lad. Crying for something that was missing. And one night parked in my sleek coupe out in front of the women's dorms with Beverly — who was now wearing my engagement ring — I just wept and wept as I told her, *"Beverly, there's just something wrong in my life. And I don't know what it is. But there's something missing inside. Life just can't be this empty! And so I'm just going to quit school and go find whatever it is that's missing. Somewhere. Somehow. Or I'm going to die trying!"*

And I almost did. Many times. Even at my own hands.

But I was pretty good at building racing engines by this time and I had raced my coupe at the drags just often enough and successfully enough that I was getting bitten real hard by the racing bug. And boy was it exciting! The deafening scream of thirty big full-house mills turning six grand on 90% nitro down the straight-away of a one-third mile asphalt track, and the wild acrid smell of fuel and rubber and asphalt, and the screaming grandstands on their feet — will fill the biggest hole in the world.

At least for a moment.

18

And so I went to work in the service department of Huskamp Ford Company in Coral Gables, just so I could get into that frenetic racing fraternity. Just so I could scream down those straightaways and shudder around those 5G turns and see the roaring crowd behind the man with the checkered flag. And it didn't take me long.

Oh it was a little humiliating at first. Me, the big man on campus, the son of the richest dentist in town, now nothing much more than a grease monkey in a Ford garage.

"But that's all right." I promised myself. "I'll show them. Wait till I get to be a big time driver. Wait till I'm another Juan Fangio or Tazio Nuvolari. And I'm going to make it. *They'll see!*"

And I threw myself into my work and into building racing engines and cars with an absolute frenzy. I was always the first one at work and the last to leave. I was sharp and fast and never slowed down. And I was out at the track every race night, in the pits, showing everybody how smart I was and what a big time driver and mechanic I was. And then one night my big chance came.

"Hey Neill, how about driving for me tonight?" Gregory urged me. "Norman's just not winnin' enough races and I'm sick and tired of losin'! And if we don't start winnin' real fast we're gonna lose our sponsor and be outa the game. *But you gotta win and win big. And tonight!"*

I had lied to Greg and told him I had been racing all over the country, and so he thought he was getting a real seasoned pro wheel man. But I had never even been inside a big car before. But I was not about to let him know that. And I was not about to lose. No matter

19

what the cost! And as I crawled into the throbbing number 280 as her throaty big engine idled in a pulsating roar there in the pits of the Medley Speedway in Miami, I was a big man again. Number 280 was the fastest car on the track, and the sponsor, Seminole Tile and Marble Company, was willing to pay a big bonus for every event with a first place whether it was qualifying, elimination or main.

Yet I only had six practice laps in which to learn that bomb before entering the first qualifying event, and so as I roared out of the pits and into the number four turn I guess my blood must have been fifty percent adrenaline! And I stayed high up on the outside for the first couple of warm-up laps.

But then I stuck my foot in that big carburetor and never took it out until after the six were over! I qualified with a time nobody had ever turned there at Medley before! I threw that car through those turns with the engine wide open, only braking with my left foot, like no car had ever been driven there before.

Because I didn't care one bit whether I lived or died.

As long as I won.

1 was either going to be the fastest driver in the world or they would have to scrape me off the wall trying.

"Damn it Neill, slow down! Are you crazy!" Greg screamed at me over the din as I loped into the pits after the warm-up. "You're gonna kill yourself and everybody else out there at that speed! And don't push those cars on the straightaways and dump 'em out of the turns. I saw you! Now damn it, take it easy!'

"Yeah, sure." I laughed to myself. "But he hasn't seen anything yet!" And he hadn't. Because when you're as hollow inside as I was and when you're as desperate and frantic and crying out and screaming inside as I was — you'll do anything to fill the emptiness. *Absolutely anything.*

"And the thing I'm going to do," I vowed to myself, "is win! I am going to win!"

And I did.

When I got out there moments later in that first qualifying event I stood that crowd on its ears! Nobody sat down during the whole race. I lapped the field and was so far ahead of the next car behind me I lost count. And I just held it wide open, full bore, blasting my way through the traffic the whole way! I went outside the other cars and under them and between them just like they weren't even there. I guess I must have spun out ten other cars coming around the turns in that first race and I broke every unwritten rule on the track.

I was desperate and hated. But victorious.

And after that first race a dozen other drivers and owners were only kept from jumping me there in the pits by the police officer who rushed up to my aid as I climbed out of the car. And they made all kinds of vows about getting me and about killing me out on the track. But they could never touch me, and I went on that night to take every event.

And I kept on winning and winning, and in a few months I became top money winner there. And all the stag chicks who hang around race tracks were always coming back in the pits after the races wanting my autograph and wanting me to give them a lift home. And my name was always in the paper and in the racing magazines.

I forgot all about lovely little wild orchids and love and joy and peace. Because I had thrills instead. And a big bright shining future roaring around the world with fast cars and fast women.

But then in August 1952 I got a telegram one day which started off, *"Greetings from the War Department!"* And it said something about being chosen to serve my country. But I knew what it was, and I guess I never even read the rest of it. I was being drafted into the Korean War! Just as I was getting close to the top of a great career as a race car driver the rug got pulled out from under me.

But though I couldn't see it from where I was standing, my crystal ball held a whole new life as a United States Marine clear around on the other side of the world. A new life filled with excitement and tragedy. Laughter and horror.

3   "THOSE FARAWAY PLACES"

"Give me another beer and another dollar's worth of quarters, will you?" I asked the bartender in the dimly lit lounge.

It was a melancholy little joint full of United States Marines about to get shipped off to the Korean War. It was the Enlisted Men's Club in the Marine Corps Air Station in Miami, and most of them were just sitting there drowning their sorrows. And I guess that's about half what I was doing. But the other half was sort of celebrating as I popped one quarter after another into the neon juke box and blared out the then popular lyrics. *"Those faraway places with the strange sounding names, calling, calling me."* And then I'd play the one about the soldier of fortune who was about to, *"See the pyramids along the Nile; send me photographs and souvenirs. Just remember darling all the while, you belong to me."*

And I dreamed and dreamed. . .

I guess I had always been dreaming. A lifetime of dreams which was only just beginning. Because I was to dream for twenty more years. Exotic dreams of faraway places with strange sounding names —

Tangiers, Tahiti, Singapore, Baghdad. Funny how your mind can just wander you all around the world like a magic carpet. And as I sat there sipping those beers that's what mine was doing.

I had joined the United States Marine Corps.

When I got that telegram from the War Department I showed it to a Marine Major friend and he convinced me that rather than just being a "regular old ground-poundin' dog-face soldier," I should enlist in the United States Marine Corps and really see the world.

And I had taken my physical and been sworn in that day and was just killing time until the train would take me off to boot camp in a couple of days. And boy I was going to start right in from the beginning playing the part of the big two-fisted drinking fighting tough United States Marine! So for the next couple of nights I went out on liberty in my shiny new uniform honky-tonkin' from one strip joint to another. The Red Barn and all those floozy dives out in Hialeah. Big Marine! About to go off to war! Step aside everybody!

And just as hollow inside as a rusty old tin can.

But I was tough. Six feet two, 220 pounds, good wrestler, fair boxer and lifted weights all my life. I could slosh tirelessly for days through the swampy Everglades with a big rifle and heavy pack and shinny up 75 foot cypress trees to look for deer or to pick a cigar orchid out of the top without even working up a sweat. And I wanted to be tough and hard, and I wanted everybody to know it!

Then you weren't as apt to cry at night.

24

And then there was a place called Yemassee, South Carolina!

And boy oh boy, Yemassee's such a miserable little frozen swamp-island it's absolutely good for nothing. Fit for neither man nor beast. But I suppose that's exactly why the Federal Government gave it to the Marine Corps for a boot camp.

A bad place called Parris Island.

A famous news commentator had a son who hung himself there because it was so tough, and the commentator later eulogized, "If your son is in Korea, write to him. But if he's in Parris Island, pray for him!" And that's about how it was because guys were always killing themselves or drowning in the swamp trying to go over the hill.

That was the old Corps.

And our first taste of it came when the bus pulled up to pick the handful of us up there at the train station in Yemassee. A couple of the guys were smoking and lounging around as the sergeant stepped off the bus, and he lunged over *screaming* orders at them and slammed them up against the side of the bus at attention. And he made everybody throw their cigarette packs and magazines away and sit at attention in the bus, eyes straight forward, as we drove the five or ten miles to the camp. And by the time we got there we were all scared.

"All right you scum, off the bus and out here double time! NOW DAMMIT, MOVE, MOVE, MOVE!" He screamed some more.

And for the next few months it seemed like nobody ever spoke to us — they always screamed. And you weren't allowed to walk any place. You always had to run. And you never had quite enough to eat. And you never had quite enough sleep. And you never rested. Or talked. And you only went to the toilet when they told you to go.

It was tough, tough, tough.

But the worst part was you weren't allowed to flunk out. If you fell behind on the forced marches or the crawl marches which they made us do every day, or if you couldn't keep up with the endless and exhausting calisthenics we had each morning long before dawn, or if you tried to go over the sergeant's head to complain, or if you demanded to see the chaplain or doctor — they just put you back into a new beginning platoon and you had to start all over. And that just made it tougher and longer for you.

So you just had to make it! There wasn't any choice.

And after we all scrambled off the bus that first day, they ran us over to a big tile shower room where we were all ordered to strip naked and stand there at attention while they shaved all the hair off our heads. And as scared as I was you can bet I was standing there as much at attention as I could get. But I made the mistake of looking out of the corner of my eyes at a lieutenant who was walking up and down in front of us looking us over.

"What are you looking at you scum boot, damn it; do you like me or something?!" He screamed as he lunged over at me. "Answer me damn it, you scum!"

"No sir."

"Louder, damn it, you scum!" He screamed in rage.

"No sir!"

"LOUDER DAMN IT!"

"NO SIR!"

They always made us yell back our answers.

And then in the next room they gave us a sea bag full of clothing and boots before we had to run the couple of miles to the Quonset hut which was to be the home for the 48 of us for those several frantic months.

"I am Master Sergeant Dillon. I am a career United States Marine, and I am tough and I would shoot my own mother in the line of duty, and I hate every damned one of you. And you might as well understand that right from the beginning!" Our Drill Instructor growled moments later as we stood at attention by our double-deck bunks. And he meant every word of it. About thirty-eight years old and 250 pounds of steel hard killer, he had five rows of combat ribbons about his icy heart, hash marks all the way to his elbow, and a ladder dangling under his Expert Rifleman Medal proving he was an expert with every weapon the Marine Corps owned from the .45 pistol to the 3.5 rocket launcher. He was all Marine. He could do more sit-ups and push-ups and run longer and faster and curse with more filth and expression than any man I'd ever met before or since!

"And I particularly hate niggers and Jews!" He snarled as his steel eyes drilled holes in a couple of young southern blacks and a big over-weight Jew boy from New York. *"And you'll either leave here damned good combat-ready Marines or you'll stay here the rest of your damned lives! And I'll see to it!"* He yelled as he surprise-punched a big Italian kid named Tussi as hard as he could right in the belly. And as Tussi folded to the floor the rest of us tightened up as much as we could for whatever was coming to us.

And it came.

He walked up and down in front of us for half an hour punching us in our stomachs and cursing us and ridiculing and humiliating us. He went through all our personal gear and made lewd suggestions about the wallet photograph I carried of Beverly, and did the same to all the others. I remember one poor little skinny Polack kid from the Bronx who probably had dreamed of himself as a big tough combat Marine. He had cut a little article about machine guns out of a Dick Tracy comic book and had it secreted in his wallet. And Dillon just mocked him till tears ran down the poor kid's young face.

But that's how you make tough Marines I suppose. The survival of the fittest. The weak just break and die. The tough ones make it into combat and get shot and die.

But all you're really doing anyway is just killing Koreans who are searching for the same reality you're looking for. The Koreans who have the same secret kind of built-in God-shaped hole you have. The Koreans who have pictures of their wives and kids or sweethearts in their wallets just like you have.

The Koreans who cry at night just like you do.

We're all the same. Life's all the same.

But just like the screaming racing engines and the roaring grandstand, I found something there in the Marine Corps.

Maybe it was the excitement or challenge, or maybe it was the struggle just to stay alive. But it filled my emptiness right up to the top. And just like the frantic pace of the race track, I threw myself with complete and total abandon into being a big tough United States Marine. And just like the race track I made it. Whenever we ran I ran harder than anybody else. Whenever we did push-ups or sit-ups or whatever it was, I always pushed myself right to the very breaking point as though my very life depended upon that one last push-up. Which it did in a way.

Because that's all that kept me from crying.

And since I was bigger and tougher than most of the others, Sergeant Dillon made me a squad leader over twelve men the first day. And bingo — there I was a big shot again. And eating it all up.

And of course when it came to night maneuvers with a compass in the swamps I was right at home because of my Everglades training. And I had always been a crack shot with pistol or rifle, so when they marched us out to the rifle range for a few weeks of weapons training, I came out right at the top. I could make my M-l talk on rapid fire, and on slow fire, even at the five hundred yard line I hardly ever missed the black. On our final day of qualification there was only one man out of the five hundred there on the range who beat me, and that was only by one point on the five hundred yard slow fire. And he was an old moonshiner from Tennessee who was so good with the rifle it was just scary. But with the .45 pistol, .30 carbine, and .50 caliber air and water-cooled machine guns, grenade launcher and 3.5 rocket launcher, nobody beat me.

"Okay, private, fill in these papers and put down here your first choices of duty assignment." The classification clerk instructed me near the end of boot camp, for it was time for them to decide where they were going to send us for our permanent duty.

"First choice, combat line company. Second choice, combat tanks. Third choice, combat Motor Transport." I wrote.

But no, I wasn't putting in for combat duty because I was a hero. It was only because of that big hole in me. I knew I was up on a high right then with all the excitement of boot camp and hand grenades and my dream, of myself as a war hero. But like a junkie on "horse" I knew that if I didn't shoot up again real soon I was going to crash. And I couldn't stand the thought of a crash! Excitement was all I had left because I couldn't even remember those ageless jungle cathedrals or the orchids or the sweet smell of the water or moss any more.

The Marine Corps was all I had.

"You're goin' to Camp LeJeune for Motor Transport School," the D.I. laughed at me a few days before our graduation exercises, "and if you thought it was bad here, wait until you see ole swamp LeJeune!"

But I didn't care about swamps now that I was a big tough Marine. And anyway, Beverly and I were going to get married in a couple of weeks, so I didn't have a care in the world.

And a couple of days later I guess I thought I was ten feet tall as I strutted off the train there in Atlanta in my Marine winter greens with a couple of shiny new medals sticking out on my chest and my sea bag slung jauntily over a broad shoulder. And now that the little hollow rich girl was getting a big Marine husband, I suppose everything looked pretty good to her too as she ran up to me on the platform that Christmas Eve.

And two days later we walked down the aisle and promised each other that only death would part us. And we loved each other. Deeply we thought, and maybe it even was deeply. But if we had only had any idea then of the heartaches we were going to cause each other years later, we would never have wed. But after a big reception we roared off with tin cans and old shoes dragging behind on our way to the exclusive Cloister Hotel on Sea Island, Georgia. The place for a honeymoon.

But in a few days I was back up in Camp LeJeune, North Carolina, honky-tonkin on liberty almost every night with my pals and going through Motor Transport School during the days. Oh I wasn't chasing around with other girls yet, but if you're going to be a big Marine you've got to go get a tattoo and go jukin' like all the rest of the guys. And so I did.

And after several months I found myself stationed in the Marine Corps Supply Depot in Albany, Georgia, about a four-hour drive south of Atlanta, and I would commute back and forth to Atlanta on weekends so I could be with Beverly.

But soon that old gnawing was eating my insides away again.

The Marine Corps is not very exciting any more when all you're doing is stenciling numbers on the scorching hot sides of trucks all day long. Day after sweaty day in the blistering Georgia sun. You're not a hero any more. There's no excitement. And our marriage wasn't nearly as exciting as I had thought it was going to be, because they never are when you're as hollow inside as we were. And I started getting nervous and scared just like a junkie coming off a high.

So jumpy I almost killed my best friend one day.

I was taking a little catnap under a shady truck while my friend Hauptfleisch was stenciling up above. And since we used to clean our brushes and stencils in a big ten gallon tub of gasoline, he thought it'd be cute to set old Gene's boot on fire with a little gasoline while he slept. And so he did. But when I woke up and saw flames crackling a couple of feet high from my boot and saw him there on the other side of the tub laughing at me with the brush still dripping in one hand and a cigarette lighter in the other, I instinctively lunged at him in rage. I kicked the tub over on him with my good foot and touched my flaming one to his gasoline-soaked body.

"Varrroooomm!" The gasoline exploded into flame all over him as he began running and screaming! But realizing instantly what I had done, I ran after him and threw him to the ground and did all I could

32

to smother the fire with my body and my hands. And I finally got it out, but only after he had suffered third degree burns on about one-third of his body. And I stood there in the emergency clinic almost in shock as they cut his clothes and boots off of him as he screamed in pain.

"I'm sorry, Hoppy! I'm sorry, Hoppy!" I kept whispering, but he couldn't hear me. And I was scared. But when he came to and they questioned him about the fire, he was scared too. He was scared to tell them the truth — that he had set my boot on fire and that I had retaliated. So he made up some doubtful story about how he had dropped his cigarette lighter into the tub and how it had set off the gasoline. They probably doubted the story, but he stuck to it and of course I went along with it, so there wasn't much they could do. And when my Company Commander saw the huge blisters all over the palms and fingers of my hands he put me in for a medal.

Right.

Me a medal! And in a couple of weeks, in front of the whole company at attention, with newspaper photographers popping cameras away at me, the Commanding General pinned a big Commendation Medal on my chest and gave me an extra stripe, raising me from private first class to corporal.

But now I really wanted out of that place, and so in a couple of weeks when they came around with a conscription for overseas combat duty, I couldn't wait! I had put in for combat and they were dying for volunteers, so I just knew I'd be on top of the list.

"Dang it, Neill, how come my name's on the list and yours ain't!?" My country pal Farr demanded of me with a little grin. "I got a wife 'n kids 'n house, and dang it, I just don't wanna go! How about goin' in my place?" He joked.

"All right wise guy, I will go in your place, if you'll go with me to the old man and ask him to substitute my name for yours! How about that?" I surprised him.

"Let's go boy!" He grabbed my sleeve and started dragging me toward Company Headquarters.

"O.K. Neill," the Captain finally agreed reluctantly, "you're crazy and you know it, but you're on your way now, and you're off the list Farr. I'll cut your orders Neill, and you can have a three-day pass before catching the train for California." And he cracked his swagger stick on the desk top as he stood up and punched out, *'And give those damned gooks hell!"*

Ten feet tall again!

Hole all filled!

'Cause I'm on my way to being another John Wayne or Audie Murphy or Sergeant York! "Big hero," I thought as I started humming. "Those faraway places . . . calling, calling me."

"Honey, I've got some bad news for you," I lied to Beverly a couple of days later, "because they're shipping me overseas. I don't know where they're going to send me, and I sure hate to go, but there's nothing we can do about it." And as I held her in my arms and told her how much I was going to miss her, all I was thinking about was how anxious I was to get over there. *Wherever it was.* Oh, I did love her all right, but that kind of love can never fill the kind of emptiness I had.

Only God can fill that kind of hole, but I didn't know that then.

So after a troop train ride across America and a couple of weeks of tent camp at Camp Pendleton, California, and some wild overnight liberties down to dirty Tijuana, Mexico, I finally boarded an MSTS and set sail across the Pacific.

A soldier of fortune under sealed orders.

Destination unknown!

The scuttlebutt was that we would hit Hawaii and then on to Seoul. But after a couple of weeks at sea they issued us little pamphlets on Japanese customs and laws and money exchange, so it didn't surprise us when a few days later we saw the Japanese fishing junks alongside, and then finally the submarine net opening to let us into Yokohama harbor late one night.

And you know — Japan even smells exciting! There's something about the paper and the buildings and the pomade the men all wear. And the houses and bars and beer. And the girls! And when I woke up the next morning, after a dark, bumpy truck ride in the rain all night, I was on the second floor of an old Japanese Army barracks in Yokosuka. And as I opened my eyes, I almost gasped as I saw through my window the mighty and eternal and awesome and sacred *Fuji*! Probably the most famous snow-capped mountain in the entire world. And here it was looking right in my window at me!

I couldn't get shaved and dressed fast enough to fly down the steps and get going into this new life. A new life here in this strange far away land!

And after showing us all the V.D. movies and lecturing us on the staggering disease rates in Yokosuka, they sent us yelling like a bunch of banshee maniacs out the gate on liberty. *"The Yokosuka Raiders!"* They used to call us. And like Marines everywhere, we tore the town apart. And whenever we ran into sailors there were always a lot of bottles broken over a lot of heads. But just like in the movies — the Marines always won.

The ugly Americans.

And of course we blew all our money on liquor and girls and souvenirs and risqué floor shows. And a lot of guys got arrested. Some went to the hospital. And one of my pals even fell clear over his head into a honey well - a pit where they store slimy wet human fertilizer for crops. He had been running in the middle of the night out the back door of an off-limits brothel with two MP's hot after him. But when they came up to the honey well and saw him spitting the stuff out of his mouth as he stood there up to his neck in it, they just walked away laughing. And we never let him forget it!

They finally corralled most of us back in the base after the three-day pass. And after that, with the Third Shore Party Battalion combat training schedule of twenty-five mile hikes almost every day, we weren't nearly as eager to go whooping it up as we had been. The constant and very real war games we had to stage up at Nagai Beach against the UDT Company which shared our base would really wear us out. As tough and wild as we were, they were even more so!

But like a feral stallion kicking over his traces, I was always in some little kind of jam or another. Like the time I got busted back to PFC for throwing a bayonet and sticking it into a locker box. And I had no more than gotten reinstated to corporal than I was in trouble for something else. Nothing really evil, just pranks and pure wildness.

But I sure was glad they never pinned the dynamite job on me!

During a night of war games I had secretly crawled down on my belly to where our nasty platoon commander kept his jeep parked back up against a giant Japanese oak tree. And I had securely taped three pounds of TNT to the tree with a roll of friction tape and then had tied a one-second pull detonator from his back bumper to the TNT. *My oh my - was he ever unhappy about that!*

After several months I put in for a transfer and wound up in a Motor Transport outfit twenty miles west of Kyoto — the most beautiful city in Japan.

We lived in an old Japanese Kamikaze base in a little town called Okubo which consisted of one small train station, five bars and about three hundred "butterfly houses." And since liberty went from dark til dawn each day, a lot of the guys were met every evening by their little sloe-eyed butterflies who would walk them home to a warm dinner of yakamishi and hot sake followed by an evening of domesticity at which the Japanese beauties have no peers. Then at dawn each day you could see the couples coming back arm-in-arm to the gate, with fond farewells until that evening. And since you could have this comfortable little kind of arrangement for $30 a month, including food and girl and house and all, it wasn't too bad a deal.

"Hey, there goes the preacher with his little chick!" I roared with a gang of guys one evening as our chaplain headed out of his office hand in hand with his little Nipponese lovely. He kept her for the whole year and a half I was there, and the only difference between him and the other guys was that since he was paying a little more, she was a little cuter. And since he was an officer, she was allowed to come onto the base to meet him every evening rather than just waiting at the gate like all the others.

"Some chaplain!" I used to think.

But then I didn't judge him too harshly, because I spent some time outside that gate, too, although I never felt comfortable enough to make a permanent arrangement out of it. And to tell the truth, since the incidence of venereal disease there in the camp was almost 160 per cent, I just didn't spend a whole lot of time cementing Anglo-Asian relationships at all.

But I did do a whole lot of juking and night walking and all sorts of other things right from the first night I got there.

And I had only been there a few days when I fell into a real sweet duty assignment. Some big character from California had been driving one of the Army buses and was about to get rotated back to the States.

"Hey listen Neill," he smiled, "the sergeant's gonna be asking tomorrow for someone with a bus license to take over my bus, and you oughta volunteer because it's the best job in the whole place!"

"Yeah, but I haven't qualified for a bus on my license yet." I lamented.

"Well, forget that! Gimme your license and I'll get you qualified in about ten seconds." He bragged. And he did. He just typed in the words, "Bus, gas," on the appropriate blank line on the back of the license and forged some initials by it, and all of a sudden I was a qualified bus driver.

And sure enough, the next morning at muster the sergeant called out for a bus driver, and there was old Gene right up front to grab the gravy job.

And it really was. I had open gate liberty, and since I was assigned to the Army I lived in the best of the two possible worlds! Sort of in-between the two branches of the service, with all the advantages of each and none of the disadvantages of either. And for a year and a half I was all over southern Honshu, day and night, in my bus— sometimes on duty, but just as likely off on something of my own. I bootlegged a lot of Army liquor to the natives and was always riding the little Japanese girls and lonely Army nurses around town.

Then a few weeks later I whispered to one of my buddies, "Listen Larry, the other bus driver is going stateside tomorrow, and they're going to be needing a replacement driver in the morning. So give me your license, and I'll fix it up for you tonight just like mine so you can drive the other bus!"

39

And we did, and what an incredible partnership that turned out to be!

Seventeen years later the same Larry Griggs, by then a wealthy and respected building contractor from Ocala, Florida, was to walk into my plush Miami law offices with a briefcase full of counterfeit twenty dollar bills. And he was later to spend one year in solitary confinement in the Fox Hill Jail in Nassau, Bahamas, for passing the stuff over there. And after his release, he and I were to get involved in some bizarre and intricate narcotics importation schemes with some of my clients.

But while we were there in Japan in the bus business together, we were inseparable. We would taxi down to Kyoto about every other evening for a hot bath and massage in a plush little Japanese bath house; and then we'd spend a few hours in our favorite little hideaway, a cozy, strictly off-limits and exclusively Japanese lounge rather appropriately called, "The Bacchus."

And we had a great time bussing sightseeing Marines all over Japan to Nara, Kamakura, Takaraska and Tokyo and other such exotic and fascinating places. It was only $30 round trip to Hong Kong, and there was pheasant and deer hunting up in Hokkaido, and mountain climbing on Fuji, and weekends at the beach with the little Japanese pearl-diving girls. And the geisha houses and festivals and boating on Lake Biwa.

Those faraway places with the strange sounding names - calling, calling me.

But it wore off.

40

Just like a kid starting on beer, then he has to move up to liquor. Or starting on marijuana, he's got to move on to hash and then to coke and then to horse. And then to die. Because there's no place higher to go. It's the end of the line because the hole has gotten too big. Because the more you've tried to stuff into it, the bigger it's gotten.

The war had ended, and there wasn't any combat for us to dream about any more. So some of the guys went over the hill and joined the French Foreign Legion. A couple went A.W.O.L. to Buddhist monasteries. A lot of them just disappeared over the fence forever into the darkness of the little back alleys and bars and the seething throng that is Japan.

But they sent me home.

And after two sea-sick weeks in the stinking little forecastle three decks below the water line way down in the plunging and giddying bow, we coasted silently under the great Golden Gate Bridge. Back to the land of the free and the home of the brave, they say.

But as long as I was on the move, in new places and doing new things, everything went great.

And so I had a fine couple of weeks in San Francisco up on the Top Of the Mark and out in the Sinaloa Mex Cantina and down in Chinatown. But I just left my Marine Corps uniform, medals and all, right there in the clothing store, where I bought the fancy suit, as I headed to the airport the day I was released.

41

"Hi Beverly!" I smiled as I snuck up on my wife unexpectedly there in her apartment in Atlanta. *"I'm home, baby. Home for good!"* I promised her as I held and kissed her.

But time was running out for us.

Time was running out for me.

"Objection, Your Honor!" Sly old criminal lawyer Carr grinned. "The State has completely neglected to prove the chain of custody of this bag of what they claim to be heroin, and thus it is clearly not admissible into evidence and my client is entitled to a directed verdict of not guilty!"

"Your objection is sustained." The judge sighed in disgust at the green prosecutor. "And your motion for a directed verdict is granted. The defendant is found not guilty!"

"Well, old Henry pulled off another one." The bailiff whispered to me as he shook his head incredulously. *"And look at that bag of heroin!* Half a million dollars' worth, and the defendant just as guilty as hell, but old Henry got him off on another technicality! Made himself a good bundle on that one, too, you can bet. Wins 'em all and makes money faster than he can spend it! *What a life!"*

"Yes! What a life!" I thought to myself as I watched with envy as the smooth old criminal lawyer walked, poised and majestically, out of the drama-filled courtroom with his rich Italian hood client. And

people whispered and stepped aside obsequiously as old Henry flamboyantly touched the broad flat brim of his Panama planter hat with one finger, indicating his adieu. Sealing his triumph.

"Yes what a life indeed." I dreamed.

I was back down in Miami now in the small loan business with my partner Maston O'Neal, a wild ex-airline pilot and football hero and swinger who was making a bundle as a promoter. And he promoted everything in Miami from the fighter Bobby Dykes to the multi-million dollar Biltmore Hotel deal. And he always had a string of yachts and airplanes and Cadillacs, and all the little admirers who dig that sort of thing.

I had worked for a year in my father-in-law's Ford agency in Atlanta after my release from the Marine Corps, but had quit to go seek my fortune. Racing cars and dirty fingernails couldn't fill the hole anymore. It had gotten too big.

And then I had discovered the criminal courts right across from our small loan office on Flagler Street, and I suddenly found myself more and more hanging around there. Watching. And learning. And what an incredible melodrama I saw! A moving monolith of emotions of triumph and tragedy, of depravity and exhilaration. A staggering tableau of human frailty and victory. Life in its most raw and naked state, where the criminal lawyer is god!

And I wanted to be god!

So Maston and I sold out our loan business, and I went back for two more years of college at the University of Miami. I majored in philosophy and, as always, threw my whole being into the race.

Here was something I could really sink my teeth into, because I found myself studying how the greatest minds of all recorded history had searched for the same reality I had been searching for. How they had dreamed my same dreams. And I saw how Plato and Plutarch and Spinoza and Sophocles and all the other total and infinite geniuses of all ages past had cried out for something that had meaning. Grasping desperately for any piece of flotsam or jetsam before they went under for the third and last time.

Fruitlessly. Chasing rainbows.

But in my supreme ego I suppose I thought perhaps I could simply intuitively somehow find the answer. Find reality. Find the revelation no one else, I thought, had ever found before. By studying and thinking. Alone.

And like all the greatest sophists of the philosophical persuasion, I intuited certain basic premises upon which I built my logically irrefutable, yet totally false, truths of life.

Time was infinite. There was no beginning and there will be no end. You needn't pause to explain how a rose came to be because it always was. Spatial creation and evolution were nothing more than childlike fantasies spawned of immature and illogical minds.

And space? Infinite of course and of the same dimension as time, yet incomprehensibly so to our finite minds.

God? Of course not! The most childish of mechanisms.

Morality? Nonsense! "If you have an itchy spot, you scratch it!" My bespectacled and genius professor of philosophy reasonably insisted. "So if something gives you pleasure, you do it. If you see something you want, you take it. Why not?"

Oh, I was so smart! I thought.

And by the time I graduated and got ready to enter Law School in the fall of 1958, I was already starting to really play the role of the smooth operating big criminal lawyer. "Acting out," the psychologists call it. A little player on a great big stage. An empty little puppet with a big swimming pool out in suburbia and a shiny new sports car and an airplane. And a broad-brimmed Panama planter hat!

Nothing inside but raw ego to keep him going.

But by now my son Cole Morgan Neill had been born, and he was the only vital contact with reality I had left. Because I loved him so deeply and intensely. The only vital contact I had, I suppose, because I saw in him, as I used to smile down at him as he slept, that love which I had missed so tragically and painfully from my father. And I wanted to be to that sweet little boy everything my father had not been to me. But as intensely as I loved him and as stabilizing a sea anchor as he was to be in my storm-tossed next three years, he would not be able to hold my head to the wind.

I was being driven toward the reef. Storm-tossed in a black sea of dreams.

But like the roar of the racing engines and the dreams of myself as the big combat Marine hero, I again threw myself now into Law School with unparalleled intensity. I was going to come out on top! And at the end of the first quarter, like in my first car race, I had lapped the field. Straight "A" Dean's List. Three American Jurisprudence awards the first quarter for outstanding scholastic achievement. Officer in Delta Theta Phi law fraternity. When I briefed a case in class nobody ever debated or questioned me. And by the end of the second quarter, I was the undisputed leader of my class. When I was given a full academic scholarship, and as I earned more and more awards and honors, my insatiable pride filled to overflowing that secret God-shaped hole within me.

But pride is a hungry and ravenous and all-devouring monster within a man. And it will drive him like a demon to unbelievable lengths.

And so even when my loving little daughter Lydia Paris Neill came along to join Cole as another anchor reaching up to hold my lost soul to reality — I would not. I became as overbearing and intolerable and insufferable at home as at school. I nagged and demanded and drove and abused. Always grasping and climbing.

I clerked one summer for Max Lurie, a feisty little Jew mouthpiece from Chicago, and then the next summer for the Public Defender's Office, always pushing and shoving to make a name for myself there on Flagler Street and around the courtrooms. By the time I began clerking for Heflin, Milton and DeLeon my senior year, I had a pretty big image all cut out for myself. Tanned and athletic from yacht racing and cross-country bicycle trips, I flashed around town in fancy

47

clothes and started spending a lot of time in the groovy little dives where legal secretaries and airline stewardesses hung out.

And I saw less and less of Cole and Lydia. And Beverly.

And after I received my Doctorate in Jurisprudence cum laude in 1961 and breezed through the three-day bar exam, I really started getting like old King Midas. Everything I touched seemed to turn to gold, and I thought I was just about the biggest shot to ever have come down the pike. And so did Sue and Dorothy, two of the legal secretaries at Heflin, Milton and DeLeon.

And for a little extra excitement that summer I sailed my twenty-one foot midget ocean racing class sloop all over the Bahamian islands alone. A solo cruise over hundreds of miles of open seas with lots of exciting new ports and faces — like Cat Cay and Nassau and the Berry Islands. And for a week or so I lounged around there at the docks of the Nassau Yacht Haven, sipping rum punches and impressing the daughters of the rich yachtsmen with my great nautical bravado.

But my bravery nearly cost my life later. I was taking pictures of the boat while underway. I had rigged her for self-steering and was standing up on the high side taking pictures of the pilotless helm when an unexpected sea lurched the little shell violently abeam, and I started over the side!

"My God, this is it!' My mind raced madly as I fell. "And the nearest island's thirty miles away through the shark-filled Tongue of the Ocean! And the boat will just keep right on sailing away from me as I die here after hours of treading water! My God, what a way to go!"

But suddenly — without having any idea how it got there — I found myself clinging frantically with a death grip to a line on the starboard side. A line which just somehow miraculously got into my hand. I wasn't going to die after all! But I was going to wind up doing almost exactly the same thing again some eight years later, only in a smaller boat and farther from land.

But after the trip, and back practicing law at Heflin, Milton and DeLeon, I was still longing for excitement when I suggested one day, "Buck old man, what we need is one of those cozy little cabanas over there by that swimming pool." I pointed out of our office window across the Miami River to the Robert Clay Hotel and Cabana Club. "Where we can work out and take a steam bath at lunch time and a little dip in the pool. *And such!*"

"By all means, Doctor," Buck Virgel grinned as he admired the tanned bikinis lounging in the tropical sun around the lush pool area.

And the next day we were enjoying lunch by our own cabana amidst the luxuries and bikinis. But it didn't serve only as a sophisticated spot for a noon break; it became something of a home away from home. A trysting place at lunch time and in the evenings and on weekends for girls and lawyers and parties.

Buck was something of a rounder himself, as the two police officers could testify whom he slammed up against the side of their own paddy wagon the night they tried to arrest him. Because it just didn't seem reasonable to him, in his state of inebriation, that they should haul him off in a black mariah for something as innocuous as taking a little nap during the middle of the night. Though he did have to admit that at the time he was so unreasonably apprehended by the officers he was slightly au naturale and lying out on the luxuriant carpet of the hall of a downtown skyscraper apartment building. But after all — weren't his clothes neatly folded beside him?

"Listen! You two Bobbsey twins are going to have to cool it over there at the Cabana Club!" Our senior law partner Paul Heflin grinned one day at Buck and me in Paul's office. "The management over there just called me and suggested they simply do not care to have to dive to the bottom of the pool each morning after you lads have had one of your tea parties there, to fish up beer bottles, ladies' shoes and sundry other less mentionable articles of clothing!"

But a few weeks later when Buck broke into the cocktail lounge there one night to requisition a few additional brews for himself — seeing that the management had so thoughtlessly decided to close up and go home before he had completely quenched his thirst for the evening — the Bobbsey twins were ordered to vacate the premises.

I hadn't had any trouble those days with the old hollow place inside me because I had just kept it filled up with parties and girls and roaring around town in my Morgan 2+2 sports car with the dashing leather strap over the hood. And yacht racing and motorcycles and the glamour of the young barrister.

But then my little theatre closed down one day.

"Gene, you're going to have to leave this firm." DeLeon frowned at me in my office. "Just take whatever reasonable amount of notice you want to make other arrangements."

Just like that. I was fired.

Of course I knew it was mostly because I was too wild. But then I had also accused Hefiin of sharp dealing me out of $20,000 on a real estate deal I had put together on the swank Black Caesar's Forge. And then, too, one of the partners really had eyes for Sue, one of the secretaries who was following me around. But when you got right down to it, it was all the same old thing.

That old God-shaped hole!

Haunting me! And gnawing and devouring me from the inside!

And so I had to lie to the law firm of Worley, Gautier and Patterson when I applied to associate with their firm. But I had such an outstanding scholastic record and reputation as a dynamic and potentially powerful young lawyer, they thought they were getting a pretty good deal when they took me in as an associate.

And I *did* put on a good show.

At least at first. I always did at first. I worked hard and long and did some brilliant brief and research work, and they were really impressed. But of course the dynamic spurt soon waned, and I was again climbing the walls. Looking for that vague something. Whatever it was.

And then it really happened to me!

"Gene, this is Beverly." I got the tragic call in my office one day. "Can you come out here to the City of Miami jail and get me out? The kids

are with me here. *I've been arrested for shoplifting from Burdine's."*
She intoned coldly and unemotionally — almost trance-like.

And as I tore out of the office, I shouted to the cab driver, *"There's an extra twenty in it for you if you can get me there in five minutes!"*
So he roared away from the curb and careened out toward the jail some five miles through downtown Miami traffic. My heart pounded and my hands and feet grew numb and cold as I visualized Cole and Lydia there in jail. In my mind I saw them going through the brutal humiliation of the arrest in the swanky department store. I knew how sadistically some of those store detectives abuse everybody, and my heart cried out for my two babies. My two anchors.

Later I felt dazed as I led the two of them away from the police there in the station and put them on a bench outside to wait.

"Daddy, where's our mommy?" Little Cole cried. "Why have they taken her away?"

"It's okay, baby. It's okay." I cried as I tried to reassure him. But my heart felt torn from my chest as I said, "You wait right here and take care of Lydia, and I'll go back in and get mommy."

"We can release her in your custody, Mr. Neill," the booking sergeant smiled understandingly, "but only if you'll get some judge on the phone to authorize it."

I must have frantically called a half a dozen judges before I could find one in his office to speak the word for her freedom. But I finally did, and after Beverly was booked and mugged and fingerprinted, and as I later put the three of them in a cab and watched as they drove away for home from the police parking lot, I felt like my whole life had crumbled down on me.

Beverly was going to jail, I thought, and I felt limp and dead.

When I got back to my law office I cried like a baby as I told one of the partners what had happened.

And as Beverly and I waited in the sweaty Miami Municipal Courtroom for her trial a few days later, along with the drunks and prostitutes and junkies and burglars, I was humiliated and broken and empty, because I knew she would probably have to do ten days or so in the Dade County Stockade. And I knew it would absolutely break the kids' hearts. And therefore mine.

The Stockade was a wretched place for the men or for the women. *And I wonder what I would have done right that moment if I had known that nine years later I would be a maximum security federal prisoner there with fifty years to serve!*

But I guess I never did worry much about Beverly. Perhaps because it didn't seem to bother her at all. She had never even cried there in the police station. She hadn't shown any emotion about it at all. She didn't even seem to regret it as we sat there waiting to be called up before the judge.

"Beverly wanted to be caught." The judge frowned up from the psychiatric report. *"Because of her unfortunate marriage."* The words echoed through my memory for years. "And Gene," the judge continued gravely, "this is not the first time she has shoplifted at Burdine's. She's been doing it for some time now and has been returning the stolen items for money refunds. They can prove it. And yet you have a charge account there and a couple thousand dollars in your checking account!"

"But based on this psychiatric report," he continued softly, "I am going to withhold adjudication and sentence, and give you an opportunity to rehabilitate her. *But you are going to have to really do something right now. Or she'll be back here soon.*"

"Do something." I kept repeating to myself as we drove home. But do what? What? What?

So Beverly and I separated and she went back to her folks in Atlanta.

And she took my only two anchors with her.

I wished I could die, and I thought about killing myself. I even got out my .45 and with a shell in the chamber I cocked it and put it to my head and cried and cried as I tried to pull the trigger. *Oh how I wanted to die! Because my heart was already dead!*

But it just wouldn't go off.

And so I went back to my office and tried to practice law. But I was too dazed to even think. And too lonely and empty. And I cried every night. And when I would see toys in a store window I would think of Cole and Lydia and start crying right there on the street.

And I began drinking more and more.

But then I hired Dorothy!

Little vivacious married teeny-bopper red-headed hot-tempered Dorothy — whom I had seen so much of when she was working as a legal secretary over at Heflin's office. The same Dorothy who had danced with me over at the Cabana Club. Who seemed to somehow understand why I cried so much. Who always seemed somehow to secretly know what it was going to take to fill that God-shaped hole.

The same Dorothy who is now helping me type this book.

But Dorothy was divorced now. And she had rented a little apartment which was right on my way home from work, and I began spending a good bit of time there in the evenings and on weekends. Mostly just searching time. Looking for myself, I suppose. Looking for something to cling to.

And then late one night, as I let myself into the silent blackness of my back door, I sensed somehow that *I was not alone!* The stillness and total black were eerie and chills began to creep down my spine. Then as I stood there in the kitchen by the back door I suddenly became aware of the soft sound of footsteps coming toward me on the terrazzo from the dining area. And I froze. Ready to spring.

"Gene do you want me back?" Beverly shocked me as she flooded the room with light with the switch by the door.

The impact was tremendous.

"Beverly, I just don't know!" I stammered. "I just don't think I love you anymore. I'll just have to think about it. I don't know. *I just don't know! I know I'm miserable and empty and lonely. But I just don't know!"*

55

She didn't argue or ask me to take her back. In fact she simply turned and walked silently out of the room.

But after she had gone to bed in another part of the house that night, I hastily threw a couple of arms full of my clothes out on the bed, tied the sheet around them and left. I crept out and pushed my Vespa motor scooter down to the corner before starting it up, so she wouldn't hear me.

And I left.

And I went clear around to the other side of the world. Clear around to the other side of the world to find the answer. To another one of those faraway places with the strange sounding names to find the answers I'd already searched the world over for.

To try to fill that God-shaped hole.

To try to be free!

56

5   PARIS IN THE SPRINGTIME

"Paris!"

An electrifying word!

A word which utterly intoxicates women with heady thoughts of provocative new fashions and titillating perfumes and golden bubbling champagne! And romance! A word which inflames the hearts of men around the world with exotic thoughts of sultry young Parisienne girls and roaring sports cars and sidewalk cafes and the glare and blare of the Pigalle. And romance! And of course there's the *Louvre* and *Notre Dame* and *La Tour Eiffel* and *Les Champs Elysees* and the *Montmartre* and the incredible river Seine and on and on. . ..

Ah Paris! The most beautiful city on planet earth! The world capital of art and literature and music and culture and love! Dating all the way back through the ages to times unrecorded.

And there I was circling above this timeless never-never land as my plane began descending for a landing. And I thought how very far I had come since I pushed my Vespa motor scooter out of the garage back there on the other side of the world.

A lifetime away!

I had driven over to Dorothy's apartment that night, and then the next morning, without giving notice to Worley, Gautier and Patterson or to anyone, I had bought a cheap suitcase and had withdrawn the money in my bank account and had run! I didn't even tell Dorothy where I was going. Or my poor mother. I guess maybe I didn't even know myself for sure where I was going. I only knew I had to get out of that house. And out of Miami.

And I couldn't get away fast enough!

It was as though I were in a nightmare — desperately trying to run and screaming and crying to get away from some fiendish force. Trying in sheer terror to escape. Yet in vain. Held back by some unseen hand. Unable to move.

I had taken a bus to New York and then had caught a London plane. And as I had sat there miles up in the air above the bottomless North Atlantic I had shuddered to myself, *"My God! I have really burned my bridges behind me this time!"*

And my heart had pounded and my face had flushed as I thought, "But I'll just stay in Paris. I'll just live there the rest of my life. Start a new life there. Maybe somehow I can find that peace I've been looking for so desperately. I'll just get a menial job of some kind. Carpenter. Truck driver. Anything! And maybe after a few years I'll be able to forget Cole and Lydia. And everything."

58

"No! I'm not running away from myself!" I argued with my absent brother's haunting accusation. "I'm only trying to find some kind of happiness somewhere. Peace."

And I truly was not running from myself. I was only trying to find that missing ingredient. That tiny key. That simple little answer that would fill my great big hole.

And as I had dashed from the plane through the freezing night drizzle to the warmth of the terminal there in London, I had wondered if Paris were going to be similarly foreboding and repelling.

"Well, in American dollars, sir," the pretty little cockney information lass had brogued, "it's about four dollars by jitney to the nearest hotel and they will charge you about twelve dollars for the night. But indeed I simply can't tell you when I shall be able to seat you on a flight to Paris, for all reservations are filled for the next several days. But if you will be there at the post tomorrow morning at 5 o'clock sharp, I shall see what I can do for you."

As I passed the lonely night pacing the floor there in the terminal and napping a few moments in a chair, my mind had been torn back and forth from Cole and Lydia to Paris. From Beverly to Dorothy. From death to life.

Perhaps the little lass had seen the sorrow in my eyes the next morning, for she had secretly slipped me ahead of some others aboard the Paris flight. And as we had broken through the dawn over the English Channel and had soared up into the early slanting rays of the sun above the white cliffs of Dover, I had begun watching

59

the enchanting French countryside below. It had seemed so peaceful, lying there serenely in the morning dew. Wrapped in the arms of the warm golden sunrise. Aglow with flowers and cattle and just smiling up all green and pretty at me!

As the plane banked over the *Forest of St. Germain* on the downwind leg of the landing pattern, I could see the Eiffel Tower, like something in a dream, stabbing up into the sky. And thrusting up majestically beyond the Bois de Boulogne, I could see Napoleon's *Arc de Triomphe*. And then the *Sacre Coeur! So magnificent!*

Later, I gazed about almost in awe inside the mammoth Orly air terminal while I stood there checking through customs. And I had a feeling that *maybe* I had found my home!

Paris was warm and friendly and new and exciting and so very different! Miami seemed like a vague, long-past memory out of some half-forgotten bad dream. As I hopped aboard the six franc bus for the long ride into the *Invalides* air terminal on the left bank of downtown Paris, what I saw along the way literally filled me with excitement! The quaint little shops and the centuries old cobblestone lanes beneath the luxuriant canopy of chestnuts. The endless number of lovely little sidewalk cafes and pastry shops and street vendors. And the world famous poster-covered kiosques. And everywhere were tulips and rhododendrons — and lovers.

And the street cleaners! Paris is the only city in the world which gets thoroughly hand-scrubbed each morning. Four thousand little bereted Frenchmen come out in their blue overalls onto the cobblestone streets at dawn each day. They turn on the fire hydrants and scrub the streets and sidewalks down with handmade twig brooms, and run the trash and water down into the sewers. And Paris sparkles like a jewel in the early dawn!

It's also the only city in the world where only rubber or plastic trash cans are permitted. The metal ones make too much noise! *Ah, sensitive Paris!*

And who else has the inimitable little *pissoir!*

"Bonjour, Mademoiselle." I tried my French on the winsome little Parisienne behind the information desk where we disembarked the bus. *"Comment allez-vous?"*

"I'm just fine this morning, sir," she laughed at me in her perfect Cambridge English, "and how are you?"

"Well, I'll be all right after I get over my embarrassment." I chuckled as I asked if she could direct me to an inexpensive place to live. And when I told her I thought I was going to make Paris my home she lit up with delight and jotted a name and address on a slip of paper.

And as my ancient Citroen taxi lurched along the Seine and whipped down the Blvd. St. Germain, I felt as though I were back on the race track once more! Those otherwise absolutely marvelous Paris taxi drivers develop an utter speed psychosis as they honk down the narrow, twisting cobblestone lanes, totally oblivious to the mass of pedestrians and bicycles and motor scooters and other equally insane taxis. So it was with a considerable sigh of relief that I stepped out onto the curb and looked up at my new five-story home. Three hundred years old and looked every minute of it, with its barrel tile roof and balcony windows of the 17th century.

But at this point in my sojourn, I discovered that almost no one on the Left Bank speaks English, nor is willing to, even if he can. And this included my medieval inn keeper, who had some difficulty penetrating my language barrier to explain the rules of the inn:

"The room will be $1.24 per day," he smiled in his melodious old French, "and your room will be facing the street on the fourth floor. If you want a shower, it is on the next floor down from you and it will cost 25 cents each time you use it. Whenever you do wish to use it," he continued, implying that he did not expect that to occur too frequently, "come and get me and I will unlock it for you. Then when you are finished, come and get me again so that I may lock it. There is one toilet on each floor, but you must provide your own toilet tissue. Now come with me."

And as he trudged before me up the incredibly ancient and worn old oak stairs to show me my prospective billet, it gave me pause to contemplate the feet which must have trod these very steps since long before Cardinal Richelieu or Victor Hugo. And the room was right out of the Reformation! About 16 by 20 feet of old-world charm and simplicity and cleanliness. From the ageless oak parquet floor to the rough unbleached muslin sheets, it just reached and pulled you in with its richness and warmth. But you could easily see that the electrical system and plumbing were afterthoughts added centuries after the construction. And there, gleaming in all its majestic splendor almost in the center of the room, was the indispensable and frequently misunderstood yet forever ubiquitous — bidet!

Ah Paris!

"How absolutely lovely!" I thought later as I sat there at the window sill gazing out at the whole new world which I saw unfolding below my window. The little sidewalk Cafe Le Vulnet across the street where I was to smile away so many months. The centuries old winery next door with the old-time coopers singing their Basque folksongs as they hand-carved the thick oak wine barrel stays with ancient but razor sharp drawknives. The medieval little park next to the winery with the Metro subway entrance leading down under the rich green sod. The tiny carnival-like lottery stand on the corner with the sharp-eyed octogenarian lady who always had such a warm word for me. And all the charming dark-age buildings down the block, leaning out over the timeless cobblestone Rue Linnet.

The poet who laughingly penned the lyrics, "How you gonna keep 'em down on the farm after they've seen Paree!" had to have been there! For indeed it is utterly hypnotic and enchanting!

So after I had taken my first of many money-saving baths in the bidet and after I had brushed my teeth and shaved at the sink on the wall behind the old folding screen, I raced down the stairs and across the cobblestones to the cafe. And I excitedly ordered the most common of all Paris breakfasts - bread and butter with red table wine - though some of Parisians substitute the half-and-half cafe au lait for the wine, and the more expensive croissants for my French bread.

The dozen or so Frenchmen who were there lingering over their wine or iced Pernot or coffee literally opened their arms and drew me into their world. No city is more friendly than Paris! And they instantly made me a part of their lives and families there in the Latin Quarter on the Left Bank of Paris.

On a different planet from Miami.

There was the always-smiling old grand-pere who was the elder patriarch, and his son and daughter who ran the cafe. And there was the building contractor and the English teacher and the airline steward. Even a Paris gangster, who took to me so warmly. And the workers from the winery. Only the English teacher spoke a word of my language, yet I melted into their lives as though I had never been anyplace else. Every morning I would sit there with them, soaking up their camaraderie, and promenade with them in the evenings from one cafe to the next. And watch them giving all the girls a tumble and laughing at their boldness. The national sport of France!

"Today is Bastille Day!" My handsome young building contractor friend excitedly exclaimed to me in French as he enthusiastically hugged me the morning of July 14, 1963. "And tonight! Ah, my unfortunate American friend, you have not yet lived until you have walked the streets of Paris on the night of Bastille Day! Paris will be aflame with fireworks! And all the girls will be aflame with romance! And in the streets there will be love-making and dancing and drinking and merriment all night!"

"Rest today my good friend, for tonight I shall show you the real Paris!"

64

And indeed he did!

Except he understated it! For it makes our somewhat similar 4th of July look like one tiny old firecracker.

It starts along the Seine at dark with what has to be without any question the loudest and most incredible pyrotechnical display on earth! For what seems to be hours, Paris is lit up as bright as day by continuous ear-splitting, multicolored, earth-shaking fireworks! There are bands playing and throngs of people dancing in the streets! And all the girls of all ages are looking for boys. And the boys for girls. And it goes on and on through the night. The poor little street cleaners have thousands of tons of wine bottles and streamers and debris to sweep up at dawn as the last of the revelers stagger homeward!

Ah Paris!

The next day I must have walked ten or twenty miles in my Levi's and Indian moccasins - up to *Blvd. Montparnasse* and over to hoary old *Blvd. St. Michel*. Across *Ile St-Louis*, one of the two tiny islands in the middle of the *Seine*. Then to *Rue de Rivoli* and on to the world-renowned *Ave des Champs Elysees*, stopping only for lunch at a sidewalk cafe beside the unbelievable *Etoile*! The most spectacular of all Paris' rond-points where stands Napoleon's staggeringly powerful and seemingly eternal *Arc de Triomphe!*

I drifted through the day along the ancient quais and into the beguiling little side streets. I strolled along the romantic *Trocadero* and under the overpowering *Eiffel Tower*. Over to majestic Place de la Concorde and then on into the carnival Tuileries and down to the

65

largest palace in the world, the 500 year old Louvre, the art center of the universe. I ambled down the *Place des Voges* into the warm *Luxembourg Gardens*, then over to the imposing Opera and up the dizzy little ways and steps to bohemian Montmartre!

And as I sank exhausted but snugly into the feather mattress of my massive and ancient oak bed that night, I drifted off to a pleasant dreamland of sleep. A happy dreamland that was to be mine for many months. A dreamland where I would get up each morning to go out and intentionally lose myself in the magnetic maze which is Paris.

Yet it was only a dream.

But I arose excitedly and early the next morning to the sounds of the street below my open window, and spent another day exploring the narrow ways of the Left Bank and the grand boulevards of the Right. I stopped at lunchtime in a sidewalk cafe for a sandwich and a glance at the help-wanted ads in a large French language newspaper. But there was nothing for me that day.

So rather than taking my dinner in a restaurant that evening, I purchased a litre bottle (slightly more than a quart) of rich red table wine for twenty-six American cents and a long, still-warm loaf of incomparable French bread for twelve cents. I was going to have to make my few remaining dollars stretch a long way. But in Paris you can buy more calories and taste per franc in wine and bread than any other foods. So this was to happily become my staple diet until my income could begin.

And for another day or so I dreamed happily along through the cobblestone streets and forests and under the bridges and through the subways, soaking in and relishing and delighting in the sounds and smells and tastes and touches of ancient Paris. *And I had never been happier!* My past was gone! And the emptiness was gone! I was living in a storybook land of excitement and laughter! And I began writing to Dorothy to share with her all the joy of Paris, though with all my new friends, particularly from the Alliance Francaise, where I had begun French classes every evening, I wasn't yet a bit lonely.

But as the days raced into weeks and then months, I still had not found work, and my reserves were dwindling precariously.

I had made application for the indispensable working papers, *the carte de sejour* and the *carte de travail,* in the dusty little government offices, and I had even placed a French language ad in the paper:

American lawyer with some French seeks permanent employment in Paris. Hotel de Londres. 33 Rue Linnet.

And I had chatted about possible employment with some of my new Parisian friends and even with an international law firm on Rue St. Honore.

But still no job and still no work papers. And I only had a few dollars left. Yet I wasn't really worried about the money for I knew that as a last resort I could always go out and get a job unloading trucks like some of my German classmates at the Alliance Francaise or washing dishes like my Russian friend, for the officials seldom checked work papers. And after four months my conversational French had become quite fluent.

Yet it had begun!

The loneliness. Loneliness, I suppose, mostly for someone to just love me. It's so terribly lonely when you're not loved.

And the all too familiar gnawing feeling began again inside. Slowly and insidiously. But unfalteringly. I could feel it coming, though I pretended my very best I could not!

So I sat down one night and wrote to Dorothy. I told her I loved her and that if she loved me and would take me just as I was there in Paris, I wanted her to come to me. And I promised her that, for better or for worse, I would be with her and take care of her forever. But that if she was going to come to me, to catch the very next plane. And if she wasn't, to just not even answer my letter.

And then there she was! Trudging up to Customs there at Orly airport that Sunday with her heavy suitcases containing all she owned. And a great big laughing smile on her face that told me she and I were going to conquer the world together!

And indeed we were going to one day.

But only after a divorce and a whole lot of years in hell.

But as I kissed her and held her there in the middle of the terminal, I guess we looked just like all the other ever-present lovers of Paris. For everywhere in the city people of all ages are always kissing and hugging and walking with their arms around each other. Kissing on the park benches and under the bridges and in the woods and parks, and on the sidewalks. Paris is the city of lovers. And we were lovers.

And I couldn't wait to show her my city! So after we got off the bus there at Invalides, we checked her bags and strolled with our arms around each other across Quai d'Orsay to the Seine, where we just stood holding each other silently and watching the ageless river with all its barges and quaint water traffic.

Then we dreamily ambled on across to the Right Bank and the vast and majestic Place de la Concorde with its gigantic sculpted Marly horses and fountains and the seventy-five foot high, seven hundred year old Luxor obelisk. We could almost visualize the shroud and pall which must have fallen over the onlookers as the guillotine thundered down there daily on this very square during the French Revolution.

Then on up to the Champs Elysees, and a sandwich *jambon et fromage avec lait froid* (ham and cheese sandwich with cold milk) in a little sidewalk cafe at *Rond Point*. It seemed we could have sat there forever watching the fascinating city pass by.

But we strolled on - all the way up to *the Place de Etoile* and under the 164 foot *Arc de Triomphe*, and then back down to the Left Bank and a taxi from *Invalides* to our home at 33 Rue Linnet.

"I'll bet I can find a job in one day!" Dorothy laughed at me the next morning as we tallied up our combined reserves to about $150. *"With or without working papers!"*

"You're on," I said as we raced over to the Metro entrance across the street. And as we flew along under the Seine in the silent "luxury" of the rubber-wheeled George V subway, we marveled at Paris' incredible rapid transit system.

"I know just the job for you!" The lovely Parisienne secretary exclaimed in answer to our inquiry. We were up in the American Chamber of Commerce building, and Dorothy grinned down her nose in triumph at me as the girl dialed the phone and inquired excitedly in French to another secretary on the other end.

And Dorothy won the bet. The next day she started as a secretary for a big American engineering firm with offices right on the Champs Elysees. And at $65 a week American - which was a lot of money in Paris! Her boss was willing to hire her without working papers because he could carry her on his books as a temporary secretary, thereby getting around the strict alien labor laws.

"Come on!" I grabbed her the next afternoon and started pulling her down the Champs Elysees as I picked her up after work. "I've got a surprise for you!"

I had bought a plain little gold wedding band for $16 in a tiny shop on the Place de la Opera that afternoon, and had it hidden in my pocket. And during the entire three miles, as we walked to the Ile de la Cite, she begged me to tell her my secret! But even after we had entered the overpowering silence of the eight hundred year old *Notre Dame* Cathedral and I led her over to a quiet little corner of the nave there in that unbelievable sanctuary, with its fabled rose windows and flying buttresses and gargoyles—she had no idea why we were there.

"Dorothy, I love you and I would like for you to be my wife." I vowed to her as I held her hands there in mine and looked down into her shining blue eyes. "Do you love me?" I asked.

"You know I do, Gene!" She smiled back seriously. "With all my heart! Why do you ask me that?"

"Because I want you to wear this wedding ring for me forever; and I want this to be our wedding day." I said as I smiled through the tears that were welling up in my eyes. And as I put the ring on her finger, and we cried and kissed each other there in that ancient cathedral, it became our wedding day!

And that evening we had a wedding feast of grand proportions. We splurged and went to an expensive and secluded little restaurant down by the Seine, where we ordered their specialty entree of Chateaubriand, a thick juicy slice of perfectly selected and broiled tenderloin served with the inimitable Parisian sauce. And red wine.

Of course red wine! No civilized person would ever think of enjoying an exquisite Parisian Chateaubriand with any liquid other than an excellent red French wine!

But then Dorothy was a little farm girl from Missouri who didn't drink wine and who wanted milk with her dinner.

"*Mais non! Mon dieu!*" Our polished French chef obdurately refused with an oath. No one would eat his Chateaubriand with ordinary

71

cow's milk! And it looked for one tense moment as though the little red-headed farm girl and the stately chef were going to cause an international incident. But with a huff and a snort and an upturned nose the chef finally relented by not too politely placing a glass of milk in front of Dorothy. And our wedding was complete.

And every day after that I would ride with her to work on the Metro, and then spend the rest of the day walking around Paris, job hunting and sightseeing. I still had not been issued my work papers, and as the weeks slipped past I must have trod every little back street and boulevard of Paris. And I must have dreamed on every beautiful bridge and rested on every lovely little bench in the entire incomparable city. I strolled away those months all the way from St. Ouen to Pantheon and all the way from Montreuil to St. Cloud. Tirelessly and happily.

In the afternoons I would be waiting for Dorothy after work, and we would walk endlessly with our arms around each other drinking in the heady and exciting *joie de vivre - the joy of life* - in transcendent Paris!

On weekends we would stroll through woods and race up the giddy steps to Montmartre and thrill at the sunsets over Paris from the steps of the Sacre Coeur. Doubtless the most beautiful evening view in all the world. We played on the *Eiffel Tower* and along the little ways of Toulouse Lautrec's Moulin Rouge all the way up to Van Gogh's house at 54 Rue Lepic. We thrilled at the seven hundred year old *Sainte Chapelle* and the indescribable and unearthly beauty of the 1100 piece stained glass window in the nave of its upper chapel. And there was the flower market and the bird market and the 800 year old Church of *St. Julien-le-Pauvre*. And the *Sorbonne* and the *Luxembourg Gardens* and *Montparnasse*!

Ah Paris!

And I finally got a firm job offer as a teller in the ritzy Bank of America on the *Place Vendome* starting at $45 a week, but I still had not been able to persuade the government to issue my work permits.

And then there it came again.

Just a touch at first.

But even a touch is the harbinger of the doom to come.

The old gnawing doom inside me, telling me this wasn't really it. I hadn't found it yet. And I knew that even if I were to finally get my work papers, and even if I were to finally start working — something was still going to be missing. And I knew the hole would be getting bigger.

Soon!

"Honey we've got to go back to the States." I finally told Dorothy one evening. But I suppose she had seen it in my eyes and had known those words were coming. For she accepted them with a smile. A sad smile.

"I love you Gene, and I will go wherever you want to go." She promised.

But as our plane lifted up above Paris on its way to New York, and we watched our very own little city of dreams fading away below us, Dorothy cried.

In New York, I put her on a bus for her grandmother's home in Poplar Bluff, Missouri, where she was to stay until I sent for her, and we both cried. As much as anything, perhaps, because we both knew that big hole was tearing away at my insides again.

Out of my desperation I even went down to the nearest United States Marine Corps Recruiting Office and tried to reenlist, but they said I would have to have my wife Beverly's written consent. So I walked across town to another Marine Recruiting Office and lied to try to get in. I told them my wife and I were divorced, and they even gave me the physical examination, but the commanding officer smelled a rat. And he wouldn't take me.

I was broke and jobless and hungry and desperate and alone in New York City.

I remember hearing a sidewalk preacher one drizzly cold night there in the slums, and he was saying something about someone named Jesus. And he smiled tenderly at me as I walked by with my frozen hands in my thin jacket pocket and my head down out of the sleet.

But I just kept walking.

And walking.

And I slept in the degenerate Sloan House YMCA with all the perverts and homosexuals and winos until I didn't have enough money for even one more night. And then I started sleeping in the all night-theatres until I didn't have the 40 cents for that. And then I sank down to sleeping in phone booths and on park benches and in bus stations. And looking for food.

I was empty and alone and broken, and I wanted to die.

And I cried and cried.

All alone.

6   "I CAN GET YOU OFF!"

Tony was a bad guy.

A real bad guy! Boxer. Street fighter. Killer.

He had a rap sheet as long as your arm, going back almost twenty years. Filled with violent felonies. And now he was doing time for seven robberies. And with the sentences stacked end on end there was just no way he was going to hit the streets for the rest of his life.

"Tony, if you shut your big mouth and quit lying to me I can get you off!" I yelled at him there in the interview cell of the Dade County Public Safety Department. He had been lying to me loud and long for an hour and wouldn't even let me get in a word edgewise. So I had to yell at him to shut him up. Convicts are like that. They think if they lie to their lawyers loud enough and long enough, that's going to get them off.

"And if anybody's going to make up lies, Tony, it's going to be *me*!" I shook my finger at him. "Because I know a whole lot better than you do what to lie about, and I'm a whole lot smarter than you are! And that's why I'm a lawyer and you're a convict!"

"Now let me tell you what we're going to do." I confided.

And I did. And a couple of days later there in front of Judge Gene Williams, in the Criminal Court of Record, Tony walked out the door a free man.

I had gotten him off.

I was an Assistant Dade County Public Defender now. My brother had pulled me up out of the gutters of New York by giving me plane fare back to Miami. And when Dorothy joined me there a few days later, we rented a cozy little backyard apartment out on Tigertail Avenue down in Coconut Grove.

"Hi there, Dorothy!" Bob Koeppel, the Public Defender, greeted her one day in the Alfred I. DuPont Building where she had gone to work as a legal secretary. "Where's Gene? I need some help at the Public Defender's Office, and I could sure use him if he wants the job."

And so there I was.

Back practicing law. But this time exclusively criminal law; and it was exciting and interesting and it looked like I was there to stay. And I started off in the Public Defender's Office with a real bang!

"Gene, this new Gideon case has just swamped us with appeals." Bob told me apologetically. "We've got seventy briefs already past due in the District Court of Appeals. So I'm just gonna dump the whole ball of wax on you, and you're going to have to wade in there and catch this mess up!"

And I caught it up. I had first gone over and had a conference with Senior Judge Barkdull, and we had worked out a procedural system to break the logjam loose and let the cases start flowing through smoothly. And were they ever flowing through!

In that first year there in the Public Defender's office, I handled 250 appellate matters and had a win record of 85 per cent. That's a bigger volume of appellate cases and a higher win score than most criminal lawyers attain in a lifetime practice.

But I was getting ready for something really big!

I had gotten a real taste of criminal law now, and I was excited about it. I liked getting my name in the newspapers and building a reputation for myself. And I was determined to make it right to the very top of the mountain of success!

And if I could have looked into some crystal ball right then, I would have seen that as a matter of fact I was going to make it big. Right to the top!

Within a few years I was to be one of the best criminal lawyers in Miami. Perhaps even in the South. I was to have a fancy suite of offices, and the best investigator, and the sharpest associate, and the income - and all those things which go with being a big shot criminal lawyer. Publicity and power and prestige. Influence and affluence. In fact I was to one day look down my nose at the sly old criminal lawyer Henry Carr whom I had idolized back before I had gone to Law School.

Beverly had divorced me when I came back to Miami. And my pal, Judge Ralph Ferguson, had officially tied the knot for Dorothy and me. Though we always thought of that beautiful moment in Paris as our *real* wedding day.

After the first year in the Public Defender's Office handling all the appeals, Bob Koeppel put a new man, Phil Hubbart, into the Appellate Division and transferred me over as Trial Counsel. Trial Counsel with wild little Jimmy Nasella in Judge Gene Williams' court.

And boy did we try cases!

Every morning Jimmy and I would be there in the courtroom for the arraignments and motion calendar, and then we would get into the trials. In the afternoons we would go over to the jail across the street and interview the defendants whom we had been appointed that day to represent.

Most of our trials were non-jury trials before the judge for several reasons. First of all, we had such a heavy case load we just simply didn't have time for very many jury trials. And secondly, since the judge knew we were overloaded anyway, he bent over backward to give us every possible break during non-jury trials. So our clients actually had a better chance of getting off in front of the judge than they would have had with a jury. And finally, almost all of the judges there in Miami discouraged lengthy jury trials by the simple expedient of burying the defendants who demanded trial by jury and who were ultimately found guilty.

And Jimmy and I had a great time there in court together.

Feisty little hot-tempered Jimmy was about the most theatrical lawyer who ever screamed up and down a courtroom. A seasoned five-feet-five stick of dynamite mouth-piece, he would slam his files down on the counsel table, and shout and curse in his trained stage whisper, and make dirty signs at the prosecutor when the judge wasn't looking. In fact, he'd do just about anything he could think of to get his man off. If a prosecutor started getting into a pretty good line of argument before a jury, or began making points with the judge, Jimmy would push a stack of heavy law books off the counsel table so they would thunder to the floor and cause the prosecutor to forget what he had been talking about. Oh, he had a whole bag full of little tricks.

And he hated every prosecutor who had ever been born. Particularly Mike Mason and Ellen Morphonios, who were always trying to bury everybody.

I learned a lot from little Jimmy. And I started winning cases. And I just kept on winning. Even when I got transferred into Jack Falk's division. And it was tough for a defendant to win in Jack Falk's court. In fact it was so tough that Bob Koeppel pulled the other two public defenders out of there and sent Jimmy and me in there - like the Marines to Iwo Jima. And we gave the judge a run for his money!

Like in the case of big John Baker Riddlehover, for example. Grand Dragon of the Ku Klux Klan in that area! A notorious and avowed Jew hater getting tried there in front of very Jewish Jack Falk. And with Jack always being the proper do-gooder, and Riddlehover always

81

being the infamously evil man that he was, and with prosecutor Ellen Morphonios trying her very best to put another notch on her gun — old John Baker Riddlehover didn't stand a chance!

His crime was Possession of a Firearm by a Previously Convicted Felon — which wasn't exactly like spitting on the sidewalk. The State even had video tapes of him confessing to his guilt on television the night of his arrest. And the swastika arm band and Nazi "SS" collar insignia didn't help a whole lot either.

But there was a technicality.

There had been an illegal search and seizure. The arresting officer, Lieutenant Leslie Van Buskirk, admitted on my examination that he had followed Riddlehover by car for twenty-five miles hoping to catch him in a traffic violation so that he could stop and search him.

"But did he ever commit any crime at all in your presence?" I demanded on my motion to suppress the evidence.

"Well, his left wheels did cross over the yellow line there in the street for a second." He shrugged defensively.

"You mean when he had to pull around the stalled car you testified about earlier?" I dug into him.

"Yes." He admitted sheepishly.

"Did you give him a ticket for any traffic offense?"

"No."

"Have you ever stopped anybody else and given them a ticket for their wheels going over that line?"

"No."

"You just stopped him because you knew he was John Baker Riddlehover and you wanted to search his car—isn't that right lieutenant?"

Yeah, I guess that's about right."

And so Judge Falk got shot out of the saddle on that one. Not only did the District Court of Appeals reverse his denial of my motion to suppress the evidence, but the Appellate Court even discharged Riddlehover altogether!

I had gotten another one off on a technicality.

And Jimmy and I celebrated.

In fact the entire Public Defender's Office did a whole lot of celebrating. Particularly on Friday afternoons when Nick Tsamoutales and Pat Podsaid and our office manager Francis Kirkland and I would slip a fifth of Vodka up into our offices on the sixth floor of the Justice Building and have a "staff meeting."

"I believe in running a 'tight' ship, but this is getting ridiculous!" The sign Bob Koeppel posted on the bulletin board silently warned us. But we just kept on having our office parties. And winning cases.

And Dorothy and I were having a wonderful time together down there in Coconut Grove. It's the Greenwich Village of Miami. A little Bohemian colony down on the bay with hippies and sailboats and artists. Since we didn't even have a car yet, we would walk in the evenings, with our arms around each other, just like back in Paris - or go grocery shopping on the bus. And we spent the weekends at the beach or out in the country or just sitting and talking. We were so much in love with each other that many nights we would sit up and talk until two in the morning.

And I became one of the best criminal trial lawyers in Miami. I remember one particular day in Jack Turner's Court when I handled twenty-four criminal trials and motions in one day.

And I had some big cases.

Like the broken old man who had been a prisoner in the Raiford State Penitentiary for thirty years for robbing a man of eight cents! And he still had to spend the rest of his life there according to his sentence. Life for eight cents! The worst part was the judge who had handed out that sentence had later been indicted for bribery and had been allowed to resign silently from his office and from his right to practice law rather than go to prison. And the prosecutor on the case had later done time in the Atlanta Federal Prison for violation of the White Slave Act.

But I got him off on another technicality.

And we had a lot of funny moments there in the courtrooms, too.

Like when Tony Bethancourt got a car thief off. Tony was another one of the public defenders. And one day he just fought and fought to get some poor slob off for stealing a car. It was a lengthy trial and harangue, but he finally beat the case. But when the defendant walked out of the Justice Building a free man, he went over and stole the very first car he came to in order to get away from there. Just hot-wired it and drove it off. But he got caught with that one, too.

And it was Tony Bethancourt's car! Without knowing it, he had stolen his own lawyer's car! And everybody thought it was hilarious.

Except Tony.

Then there was the time my zipper broke in the middle of a trial.

I had been trying a big jury case in front of Judge Falk. But when I went to the bathroom during a short recess my zipper broke. And I mean it broke while it was down, and it wouldn't zip up. And there I was in the packed Metropolitan Justice Building in the middle of a jury trial — with my fly open! My pal Marco Loffredo came into the men's room while I was working feverishly in one of the stalls with my pants off trying to get the zipper up.

"Listen, Marco," I whispered anxiously to him as I peeked around the stall door, "my zipper's broken, and I can't get it up. And I'm already late in there for a trial in front of Falk. Will you please go whisper to the judge that I've got to have a recess for a personal emergency reason?"

"Yeah. Sure, Gene." He promised.

But the dirty guy went right into the packed courtroom — in front of the jury and witnesses and the spectators and the woman prosecutor and everybody — and very loudly and majestically announced, "Your Honor, if it please the Court, Gene Neill is standing in the bathroom with his pants off and with his zipper broken, and he wants to know if he can have a recess."

Good old Marco. Anything for a laugh.

Then there was the time my fellow public defender Arthur Stark, another feisty and theatrical little lawyer scoundrel like Jimmy Nasella, got in the fist fight in Ben Willard's courtroom with prosecutor John Ferguson. And old Judge Willard threw them both in the can for a few hours until they cooled off.

And then there was that rape case where we had a whole lot of trouble playing the roles of dignified lawyer and judge. The defendant was a tiny little black fellow, and the alleged victim was a great big Amazon of a woman legally named *Cabbage Head*! I thought old Judge Ben Willard was going to fall off the bench when the bailiff called out her name to take the witness stand. Old Ben wasn't very tolerant in black rape cases anyway, and that one really taxed his judicial composure to the breaking point.

But criminal law is usually not very funny.

Those courtrooms where we tried those criminal cases, first in the old Courthouse and later out in the new Justice Building, are incredible places. Filled with tears and tragedy and sorrow and despair. Screaming sometimes. And a lot of cursing and shouting.

And a whole lot of agony. They're a great big boiling pot of emotion — with the gas turned all the way up.

And such incredible depravity!

I defended a number of men who had raped or molested their own daughters. Sometimes infant daughters. Even one man who killed scores of chickens by raping them. And lots of men who strangled for fun. Daughters who murdered their fathers, and parents who beat and drowned and murdered their babies. Incredible and impossible and grotesque murders and assaults and rapes and tortures and maiming. Mad men! Demonic forces run amuck — rampant and screaming!

And you become a part of it after a while.

It becomes your life.

You forget what a rose looks like. Or what love is. Or gentleness or kindness. Or tenderness. You don't care.

Nobody cares.

The judges or the prosecutors or the defense lawyers or the bailiffs or the court reporters. You've flushed yourself right down the slimy brown toilet into the cesspool of the criminal courts.

And there's no way back up.

You just drink more. And you grasp and climb and lie more so you can make more money and buy bigger cars and wear nicer clothes and drink more liquor. And you chase girls and play with dope and stay drunk so the filth of your existence doesn't stink so much to you.

And then there's the corruption.

The incredible corruption. The judges and the cops and the prosecutors and the court reporters and the bailiffs and clerks. They buy and sell cases like they were commodities. A drunk driving case for a few hundred. A misdemeanor for five. Felonies come a little higher. Some of them real high. And a clerk can lose a file or an important pleading, or jimmy up the dates on the back of the folder. And the court reporter can change the transcript. Just a word here or a word there can throw a case. Cops can forget the facts or the faces or be sick at home on the last trial date. Little things that'll get a man off. And a prosecutor can accidentally confuse subpoenas so the witnesses aren't there, or neglect to lay the predicate for the introduction of essential fingerprint evidence. Or fail to prove the chain of custody of dope so it can't get into evidence.

Little things.

And no one notices except the judges and cops and lawyers intimately familiar with the case. And if the judge or the prosecutor sees a cop taking a dive on a case, he can't say anything because the judge or prosecutor knows that very same cop has seen him a hundred times with his hand in the cookie jar. So nobody can rat on anybody. And no one wants to anyway.

They just want their piece of the action. And the only time there's a hassle is when someone gets cut out of a deal.

88

Like one big bolita case I remember. Hundreds of thousands of dollars were involved, and the defense attorney had filed a motion to suppress the evidence. If he won the motion it would be worth at least a hundred grand to the defendant. So the defendant was willing to lay out a big bundle to win. And the judge knew that. And the cops knew it. And the prosecutor knew it. But the defense lawyer had made the mistake of laying all the bread on the arresting officer and hadn't given anything to the judge. Which isn't smart in the trade.

"No, Your Honor." The clever Italian cop from the Vice Squad lied. "I had a search warrant all right, but I did not knock on the door. I just pulled my pistol out and kicked in the door and walked right on in."

And the sly old cop knew that kind of testimony automatically entitled the defendant to a motion to suppress. He knew it would get him off. And the judge knew he knew it. And the judge knew a lot of money had been laid on the cop to get him to admit to that kind of sloppy police work. And the judge went right up the wall!

"Bang!" He thundered his gavel down onto the huge oak bench! "There'll be a two hour recess, and I want to see the defense attorney and this State witness in my chambers right now!"

Two hours.

You know why two hours? Because the judge knew that's how long it would take the cop and the defense lawyer to get the judge's rightful share of the bribe out of wherever it was hidden and get it to the judge's bagman bailiff before the judge stepped back onto the bench.

And as a young but learning-fast public defender, I watched carefully a couple of hours later as the drama resumed in the courtroom. The judge was all cool now. A smile on his face. And as he led the not quite so smiling cop back over his testimony, he cleaned the transcript all up nice and neatly so no honest newspaper reporter could dig a bribe story out of the file. And the defendant won. And everybody went away happy. And a lot richer.

I was learning.

Then there was the big case where a judge from a Civil Court was the defendant. He had been accused of sexually molesting a little boy. And the evidence was totally over-whelming. Nobody in the courtroom had any doubt at all that the defendant had committed the loathsome act. He was guilty and everybody knew it. But the little six year old boy wasn't real sure what date it had happened. Oh he remembered it was a Tuesday and that he had run right home afterward and told his mommy about it. And all those facts were in evidence. But because he couldn't positively say from memory what date of the month that particular Tuesday was — which didn't really matter legally anyway — the judge found the defendant *not guilty*!

Do you suppose a lot of money changed hands?

But the prosecutor was too green to even know what had happened.

And I began to notice how in the big money cases the two newspaper reporters who were permanently assigned to that beat never seemed to pick up the scent as a bribe rabbit ran across in front of them. But then I saw they were in on it too. Newspapers don't pay enough to keep a reporter honest. And for a few bucks you could even get a story about one of your cases in the paper. Or for a lot of bucks, a judge or a cop or a prosecutor could keep it out.

Oh, I was learning, all right.

And I was winning cases, and getting a big name.

But nobody would bribe a public defender. I didn't have anything I could sell. And I knew I couldn't really get into the middle of all that action unless I could get into the State Attorney's Office as a prosecutor.

So I walked out of the Public Defender's Office on the fourth floor one day, and got into the elevator, and pushed the button for the sixth floor. Where the State Attorney's Office was located.

I was going up.

"LET'S BURY THEM!"

"Let's get in that courtroom and bury those bums!" Sam Kleinfeld
growled in his inimitable Brooklynese as the three of us pushed our
way through the wide-eyed throng of courtroom thrill seekers. Into
the arena! The gladiators were ready! The atmosphere was electric
and charged with excitement! There was going to be blood on the
sand today!

"Hear ye! Hear ye! The Criminal Court of Record in and for Dade
County, Florida, the Honorable Judge H. Paul Baker presiding! God
save America and this Honorable Court! Be seated please! And no
talking!" The bailiff sang out as the judge pretentiously mounted the
steps to the imposing height of his regal bench.

"This is the case of the State of Florida versus Tulio Costerelli,
Genero Gaultieri and John Matera." Judge Baker boomed in his
trained baritone. "Put the first six venire men in the jury box, Mr.
Bailiff."

The famous "Harbor Island Spa Robbery Trial" was about to begin.
The biggest robbery in the history of the State of Florida. Eight

million dollars the police said. And I was about to prosecute it —
along with two other members of the Special Prosecution Division of
the Dade County State Attorney's Office.

And it must have taken us two or three weeks just to get over the
preliminary motions and to get a jury selected. With three super-
sharp but primadonna-type defense attorneys like Dick Barest, Phil
Carlton and that crazy little Louie Vernell with his big Adler elevator
shoes, it was a wonder the case ever got to trial at all.

And the defense lawyers pulled every neat trick in the bag to stop
the trial. Or to get error into the record. Or to get a mistrial. Delay or
confusion could mean victory for them. And it was literally a matter
of life or death!

Like about the morning of the tenth day when Louie Vernell just
didn't even show up for trial at all! And believe me — lawyers just
don't do that. You don't take off for parts unknown during the
middle of a trial when the jury's almost picked and when the judge
has subpoenaed two hundred venire men for that day. 'Cause judges
will cold throw you in jail for that kind of trick.

But jail didn't look too bad at all to Louie, because he had made all
kinds of great big rash promises to his client Genero Gaultieri.
Promises like the case wasn't even going to get to Court at all, and
that big Genero didn't have a care in the world. But as little Louie
saw his promises beginning to fall apart, he began sweatin' it a
whole lot! Because Gaultieri was out on bond on the streets, and
Italians like Gaultieri take promises from defense lawyers real

seriously! So a mistrial in exchange for a few days in the cooler looked real good to little Louie right then.

But Paul Baker was no dummy. And with the newspapers and police and politicians breathing down his neck, he wasn't about to give Louie a mistrial for his misconduct. He just laid a big fat fine on him, and the trial went right on.

And the first witness for the prosecution was a slimy little creep from New York named Bruce Braverman. He was doing time in New York State, and we brought him all the way down by a couple of Marshalls, just so he could testify about a conversation he had overheard in New York. A conversation where the defendants were planning the heist.

And old Bruce was really something else!

One day a few months earlier, he had tried to pass off a counterfeit bill to the desk clerk at the super-swanky Fontainbleau Hotel on Miami Beach. But the Treasury agents had been tipped off and were standing nearby waiting for him to pass the bill. And when the desk clerk yelled for the agents, Braverman grabbed the bill back out of the clerk's hand, shoved it into his own mouth, and began to chew it up and swallow it.

And as the agents jumped on him and threw him to the floor, he began screaming, "Help! Help! I'm being robbed!" And when a number of the tourist onlookers came mistakenly to his "rescue," he slipped out from under the melee and got away!

And I wouldn't have believed Braverman on a whole stack of Bibles.

But when the jury fit his testimony in with all the other little pieces of the puzzle — although Tulio Costerelli got a directed verdict of not guilty — it was good enough for a thirty-five year sentence for Genero Gaultieri and life for big John Matera.

And now I was really a big shot! My name had been in all the papers for weeks and the television cameras were always looking for me as I came out of the courtroom. I really thought I was something!

The Special Prosecution Division of the State Attorney's Office!

I wasn't just one of the forty old run-of-the-mill prosecutors — I kept patting myself on the back — I was one of the three specially picked and seasoned trial lawyers who tried all the really heavy cases. The big publicity cases, involving well known hoods of the underworld. Organized crime figures. Mafia.

Big shot!

I had started out in the State Attorney's Office as a prosecutor in Judge Carling Steadman's court because he was probably the most defense-minded of all the judges on the bench. He was letting *everybody* off! And Dick Gerstein, the State Attorney, was furious at him for giving Gerstein a bad public image and for spoiling his win record! And since I had more criminal trial experience than almost any other prosecutor there — because of my years in the Public Defender's Office — Gerstein threw me into the arena with Carling Steadman to try to bring the conviction rate up.

But it was tough! Because good old Carling just didn't want to send anyone to jail; and he really got some kind of sadistic kick out of needling Gerstein and his assistants.

Like the time when he intentionally and publicly humiliated and vilified one young prosecutor named Chuck Sansone, until Chuck ran crying from the courtroom during the middle of the trial. Chuck was a nice young kid right out of law school who had done no wrong at all that day. Just doing the best he knew how.

But that's the kind of guy Steadman was.

But I remember one case when the newspaper editorials and TV commentators and the general public rose up in one mighty voice of protest against Judge Steadman over one case I prosecuted.

"Yes, I'm positive that's the same man!" The first State's witness testified as she pointed to the defendant seated in the courtroom by his lawyer Marco Loffredo - a lawyer who just happened to be an old pal of Carling Steadman's. "I was looking out my window that day, and I saw him trying to break in the back door of my neighbor's house! Right there brazenly in broad daylight — in the middle of the day!"

"Yeah, I received a call that a burglary was in progress." The arresting officer testified. "And when I arrived at the scene I found the defendant trying to pry open the back door with this tool which has been marked as "State's Exhibit 4A." But when I put my gun on him and ordered him to get his hands up, he bolted and ran! I chased him, but he was getting away, and I shot him in the leg. It didn't injure him badly, but it stopped him. And that's him seated right over there by his lawyer."

"When I got home from the grocery store," the little old widow lady who owned the house testified, "they told me all about what had happened, and I could see of course where the door had been all torn up where somebody had tried to break in. *Oh I'm so glad I wasn't at home when he tried to break in!*"

"Not guilty!" The Judge smiled. "Mr. Neill," he smirked, "you didn't prove the monetary value of the contents of the house! Who knows? Maybe the house was empty. And if it was, he couldn't have stolen anything even if he *had* gotten in. *So I'm gonna' let him go!* Put on the next case!"

Shot down!

And then he did the same thing to me a couple of days later when I was prosecuting a young toughie for the misdemeanor of "Possession of Alcoholic Beverages by a Minor."

"Yes," the police officer testified, "I caught this juvenile defendant coming out of the 7-11 Food Store, and he had this six-pack of Budweiser in his hands. He admitted that he had bought it in the store and that he was only sixteen years old."

"Not guilty!" The judge smirked. "Mr. Neill," he mocked me, "you haven't proved what's in those cans. Who knows? They may be filled with water! Not beer!"

98

But I instantly thought about Judge Steadman's young boozer clerk, Mike Clowe, who was seated right there in front of the bench with the big six-pack of Budweiser staring invitingly up at him from his desk. And everybody in the Courthouse including the judge knew Mike's proclivity for strong drink — and his ribald sense of humor!

"All right then, if Your Honor please," I sparred back at him smiling, "the State will call as its next prosecution witness your clerk, Mike Clowe! And I'm *certain* your Honor will take judicial knowledge of Mike's expertise in all matters pertaining to alcoholic beverages. For we all know that he indeed well qualifies, and has for many years, as one of our community's foremost imbibers."

Mike laughed and proudly nodded his head in assent.

"And we'll just have him guzzle a few cans of this questionable liquid," I continued, "and I'm sure that in no time at all he will be able to tell us whether, in fact, it is beer or water!"

"Hey yeah! Judge that's a great idea!" Mike said as he jumped to his feet and reached eagerly for the six-pack.

"Oh no you don't, Neill!" The judge frowned.

I had stolen the whole show from him, and the packed courtroom and Mike and I were laughing at him now. And he didn't like running second best.

"I forbid you to call my clerk as a witness! Not guilty! Now put on your next case!"

The truth of the matter was, I *had* subpoenaed the State's chemist as a witness — as I always did in this type of case — but he was out sick that day. And I knew Steadman wouldn't give me a continuance. So I had to try to go ahead without the chemist, assuming the Judge wouldn't make me prove that what comes in six-packs of Budweiser cans in 7-11 stores is, in fact, beer!

But I won a lot more cases than I lost. Even some really tough ones.

Like "The Case of the Vanishing Buick!"

The most intricate and entangled legal maze I ever tried as a criminal attorney. And I had to attempt to get a conviction in front of a judge who wouldn't even admit that six-packs of Budweiser contain beer!

And the defendant was really a smoothie. Brilliant! But a thief. He had bilked a number of insurance companies out of vast sums of money through his labyrinthine schemes, which he always executed with scientific perfection. Yacht sinkings. Airplane crashes. Automobile accidents. And now the missing Buick.

"Officer, someone has stolen my brand new Buick!" Jack Colson explained excitedly to the policeman who arrived at the shopping center parking lot in response to Colson's call.

"I parked it right here in this very spot and went into this grocery store and made these purchases! But when I came out, *my car was gone! And I just bought it!"*

Later, of course, he made a claim against his insurance company to reimburse him for the loss of his new automobile, and they paid him off virtually without question.

But there never had been a Buick!

Or at least Jack Colson had never owned it.

The real Buick had in fact been bought by some unfortunate gentleman down in south Florida who had taken his wife out for a spin shortly after leaving the showroom floor. But they hadn't seen the express train coming!

She was killed and he was terribly injured. And the new Buick was literally torn into a thousand pieces. Most of the car had somehow gone under the train, rather than just being hit and knocked over to one side of the track.

And sly old Colson had simply gotten the car title for a few bucks from the unscrupulous junk dealer who had wound up with the fragmentary remains of the vehicle. Then after pretending to have purchased this gleaming new beauty from the West Palm Beach Auto Auction, he had taken his new title down to some lazy and unsuspecting insurance agent who insured it to the hilt on the basis of the title alone. Without ever bothering to look at the car.

And it's easy enough to prove a murder or a robbery. But how do you prove that a car which is reported missing really is missing — and always has been!

About forty witnesses and five weeks of trial later, the jury tucked old Jack Colson safely away from insurance companies in the Raiford State Penitentiary for five years. And insurance companies and law enforcement agencies from all over America wrote letters of congratulations to the State Attorney, and the newspapers played the conviction up pretty big. And Gerstein looked like a hero.

So he moved me "upstairs" — into the Special Prosecution Division!

Sam Kleinfeld and Bill Moran were already there, and with me added we really had a quinella. Sam had retired as a captain on the New York City police force, and had then graduated from law school. He hated cons, and he made a deadly prosecutor! And at that time, Bill Moran was probably the best criminal lawyer in America. Jaunty, urbane and persuasive — Bill was without peer in front of a jury box or in digging a legal loophole out of a big stack of law books.

A dynamite lawyer!

And back in those days, when Bill and I roared around the courtrooms like young lions, neither of us would ever have dreamed that one day he would be representing me, and stand weeping in a Federal Court as I was led away to Federal prison!

But we lived pretty wild lives during those Special Prosecution days.

Dorothy and I were living on our floating home on the Miami River just downstream from the 22nd Avenue bridge. It was a luxurious two-story houseboat with walnut paneling, spiral staircase, thick wall-to-wall shag carpeting, stained glass windows and sun porches, and a cedar shake Bermuda roof. Fully equipped with a lot of liquor, Lincoln Continental, a pet parrot and, by now, two little children.

But then Dorothy and I split up. Separated. My frantic life and a little of her red-headed temper had just driven our love out the window. And she just couldn't take the pace.

But I couldn't slow down. I had to keep running.

You have to.

So to make up for Dorothy's absence, I started pitching wild parties. Like the one when Carling Steadman's clerk - my beer- drinking expert - "borrowed" the basket of pornographic movies out of the evidence room of the Criminal Court and showed them with much delight — like a Cecil B. DeMille production — up the spiral staircase on the second floor of my floating home.

Some of the judges were there. Plus prosecutors, public defenders, doctors, lawyers. Hoods. Even John Nordheimer, the crack reporter from the New York Herald Tribune. And a Miami Herald reporter named Carl Wickstrom.

And a lot of booze. And some of the cigarettes were kind of twisted on the ends and had a heavy sweet smell to them. And a few were sniffing some kind of powder up their noses.

"La Dolce Vita!" The Italians call it. The sweet life. The big time. The big shot. But hollow and empty and crying out inside for some kind of meaning in life. Searching agonizingly for some kind of reason for it all.

Always searching. Always in vain.

"Gene, I want you to try this bastard with me!" Sam Kleinfeld urged me one day. "I've tried him two times already and haven't been able to get a conviction yet! And I just don't want him to get away again - 'cause he's a filthy, slimy degenerate!"

"He hangs out in the Six West cocktail lounge," Sam continued, "where all the airline stewardesses go lookin' for guys. And when he spots some little cutie leaving alone he follows her home and watches which apartment she goes in. Then, after the lights go out and she's gotten a chance to get to sleep, he jimmies open her door and comes in on her with a knife. The dog makes her do all kinds of things for a couple of hours — at knife point — and then he leaves. All in the dark! And so the I.D. is never any good. And most of the broads make pretty lousy witnesses anyway!"

"But this time," his eyes lit up, "we've got some latent fingerprint lifts off the jalousie window — so maybe we can make him on this one!"

And we did.

We put on a couple of the previous victims for M.O. witnesses and then this victim, Connie, to give her I.D. of him. And then the fingerprint men.

And it was the fingerprints that really sent him away.

But all the way through the trial Sam and I wondered why that particular little section of glass jalousie — the one little section

104

which just happened to contain his fingerprints — didn't match any of the other dozen or so glasses in the door. It was different.

"Oh well, just a coincidence." We shrugged it off.

"Ninety-nine years at hard labor." Judge Ed Klein sealed the defendant's fate.

And so the case was over. And that was that. So the rotten bum got a lot of time. Who cares. He deserved it.

But then pretty and buxom Connie and her redheaded stewardess roommate Suzie started coming around to some of my parties and hanging around the courtrooms watching me try cases. And we got pretty chummy. And then one night Connie got bombed at one of the parties. Really bombed.

"You know that piece of glass with the guy's fingerprints on it?" She slurred.

"Yeah. What about it?" I began getting a creepy feeling.

It wasn't outa my door. Wasn't outa my door. Cops brought it. Took mine away. 'Spose I oughta do anything about that? Should I do somethin'?

No.

No, there was nothing she could do.

Nothing I could do.

That's just the way the criminal business works.

It stinks and degrades and pulls you down.

And only the inner circle of judges and prosecutors and defense lawyers and law enforcement officers are in on the corruption and the degeneracy.

Human lives are traded like kids trade marbles.

Prosecutors will let a defendant "slide" on a case. They'll let him go free — but in exchange for the life of another man! Criminal lawyers will plead a man guilty just to pay back a prosecutor for a not guilty they got the day before.

And judges will change the transcript of the record so that a man can get off. Or change the transcript so the man will go to prison. Or change a transcript so that even if a man did not get a fair trial it will appear to the Appellate Court as though he did.

One great big hoax!

The big lie!

"The toilet of the world." As Bill Moran put it.

There's no morality. Not in the bar. Nor in the State Attorney's office. Crime and corruption run wild.

Like the pass key to the Clerk's office.

Yes, I even had a pass key to the Clerk's office; and the Clerk kept the key to the evidence room lying in an unlocked drawer in his office. So to get into the evidence room, all we had to do was enter the Clerk's office with the pass key, then unlock the evidence room with the Clerk's key, and there it was: cocaine, marijuana, hashish, guns, methadrine, Benzedrine, reds and blacks, ups and downs, LSD and pornographic films!

Prosecutors would take marijuana or cocaine back into their office and have parties - right where crime was supposed to be controlled. Where justice was supposed to be meted out.

But that was too small time for me. I was going to keep on moving up.

8   ALMOST FREE

"Alfred I. DuPont Building," the expensive engraved announcements boasted. The massive bronze and marble memorial building to the elite of the Florida Bar. The yacht club, country club, international financier set of lawyers. And my offices there were exciting and expensive and impressive.

Big time criminal lawyer.

And now that Dorothy and I were back together again, and clients were waiting in line to give me all they owned to get off — I thought I was on top of the world.

And I bribed and connived and schemed and did whatever I had to do to get them off. And I don't remember a one who went to jail. Some of the big Mafia figures whom I had prosecuted as an Assistant State Attorney even came to me to represent them on appeal. Like John Matera and Genero Gaultieri.

And one day a real millionaire came to me.

"Yeah, I'll make the call for you." I said to John Sturdevant, a building contractor from the Florida Keys, "But the call will cost you $10,000 and I want it up front."

Because for ten grand I could fix cases over the phone. And I fixed his.

Then there was the one case I couldn't fix any other way than by getting the police officer suspended from his job on the day of the trial. But for a drunk driving case where the defendant is rich enough, that's as good a way to win as any.

Some of the police would even come to me for bribes. And some of the judges of the Criminal Court of Record would hint to me that Christmas time was coming up, and it sure would be nice if I would put a little something in their stocking.

Which, of course, I did.

I had made it big all right. But it was meaningless and hollow; life was empty, and I felt terrible inside. And dirty! I wanted love and joy and peace. I wanted out!

But there was no way out.

"Let's get out of here, Honey!" I said to Dorothy one day. "Let's get out of this filthy hole and just get a sailboat and sail around the world, or go down to the South Pacific and live on an island. But *let's get out of here!"*

And so it was. January 5, 1968, our sleek little specially equipped 18 foot midget ocean-racing class Alacrity sailboat coasted away from the Dinner Key dock with our family aboard — Dorothy, four-year old Heather, six-month old baby Gene and me — headed for *anywhere*.

And as I came about and started beating our way down Biscayne Bay toward Angel Fish Creek in the Florida Keys, the cesspool of the criminal courts seemed to fade quickly into oblivion.

We were almost free!

The New Day was the name of our boat, and indeed it was a new day for us. It was almost like those enchanting cypress cathedrals, with the orchids and the lovely ferns and the otters and the sunlight slanting down through the Spanish moss to the cool floor of the Everglades.

And I smiled and Dorothy smiled. And we had fun.

For a while.

But the seas were like thundering angry mountains the next morning as we pounded and surged our way giddily out into the voracious and unforgiving Gulf Stream! The shipping graveyard of the ages. The oft-times violent and angry and unpredictable Gulf Stream which thunders ever-menacingly northward along the coast of the United States to circle the ancient and deadly Sargasso Sea. Only to return and thunder its mighty course once more.

Round and round and round. The *"Devil's Triangle!"*

"My God, look at those waves!" I shouted above the gale force winds as I shortened sail down to a storm jib and handkerchief main! And I desperately plunged to the foredeck as the lower forward turnbuckle on the starboard side parted. I knew we were going to have to heave to right then or be dismasted. So we lay to a sea anchor ail that night as the gigantic seas pounded and pummeled and crashed over our little cockle shell, while the four of us lay huddled and wet below.

Oh I was an excellent yachtsman. I had sailed these seas many times before in ocean races and in all kinds of weather. And I was an excellent navigator. But the Gulf Stream will try to kill you. In the midst of storms, you are caught helplessly in the grasp of the mightiest river in the world. The ocean river.

As dawn broke I found that our half-inch nylon line had parted from the chaffing of lying to the sea anchor, and we were adrift at the mercy of sixty-knot winds and twenty-foot seas.

In an eighteen and one-half foot sailboat! With no motor!

And though we had been carried by the angry Gulf to a latitude as far north as Fort Pierce, I tried to beat our way back down to Bimini as the wind blew the tops of the waves blindingly into our eyes. And we sailed and sailed and sailed. Day and night and day and night and day and night. I took Benzedrine pills to stay awake at the helm as we were lashed back and forth by the fury of the screaming elements.

"CR-A-A-A-CK!" The tiller resounded as it broke off in my hands from the force of the mighty seas.

112

"Hand me that rifle! Quick!" I shouted at Dorothy above the roar of the wind and waves. And I jammed our little .22 rifle into the rudder for a makeshift helm.

And I steered with it and began to hallucinate from the days of ceaselessly fighting the seas under the influence of the Benzedrine. *Until the rifle gave way too!*

"CR-A-A-A-CK!" The one-quarter inch steel bolt, which held the barrel to the stock, snapped like straw under the incredible might of the waves.

I jammed our last remaining "tiller" - in the form of a two-inch oak crawfish gig - into the rudder and began steering frantically with it. And for five days and five nights I fought back at the screaming winds and seas.

But finally it was calm.

And as the sun disappeared over the watery horizon to the west, I threw an anchor down into three fathoms of sand and coral. On Mantilla Shoals!

Our incredible battle over the days had taken us back and forth and back and forth, up and down the furious Gulf Stream, until we finally had found calm and shallow water at the very northernmost tip of the Bahamian Islands.

At last we rested and slept. And though we were over threatening yellow reefs, and still had many miles to a secure harbor, I knew we would make it. And as dawn broke the next morning, our little craft

113

bobbed gently in the early morning breeze over the incredibly clear waters of the Grand Bahamas Bank.

Later, as we ran wing-in-wing down toward West End, we watched in relief and joy as the lovely underwater sights slipped below our little twin-keeled hull. The Bahamian Islands have the clearest waters in the world, and you can see a silver dollar in 200 feet of water in the out-islands. It's like sailing on air. Idyllic and delightful and lovely. Later, as we coasted under our huge Genoa into the West End Harbor, with our yellow quarantine flag flying from the starboard spreader, we breathed a mighty sigh of relief.

It took us days to get the boat back in shape and bailed out and cleaned up. And to get rid of all the now soggy food that had been ruined by the gallons of water which had poured below from the crashing wave and filled the bilges all the way to the cabin sole. But we got our strength back as we rested and regrouped there in the blazing island sun of West End. And I made a new tiller and refurbished our sleek little racer for what lay ahead.

A week later we beat once more to windward down toward the Berry Islands. We knew we had to cross many miles of open seas, but the night was fair and clear with no portent of what was to come. In the winter the Bahamas are full of surprises!

And it hit us again! Like an angry monster the winds and waves began to attack and beat us as we got out into open seas — too late to return to port. In a storm, you try and stay as far away from land as you can, or risk being driven onto deadly reefs.

114

All night and most of the next day we fought to keep our little sloop heading toward the shelter of Stirrup Cay. And as we beat back and forth for hours and hours trying to claw up into the lagoon, it seemed we would never make it. But noon the next day found us dropping hook in the lee of little Bullock's Harbor, and we fell exhausted into our bunks.

"Hey mon! Hey mon! Da captain vould like you come ovafordinna vid me now!" The handsome black native sang out in his mellow Bahamian tongue from his dinghy alongside. And as we boarded the 122 foot wooden hulled inter-island reefer, *The Bahama Seas,* the white Bahamian captain welcomed us like long-lost friends. Real seamen are like that.

"Dear Lord!" He cried, "Da seas ver so bad last night we had to bring our ship into da harbor for fear she vas going to break up in the vaves! And you mean to tell me dat you ver out der in dat little peanut shell! Dear Lord!"

We came to love little Bullock's Harbor, as once more we rested up and worked on our tiny yacht. And little black Alfred Gibson fell madly in puppy love with our Heather as they played around the beaches and coves and up the hills of the quaint little isle. At night, at anchor there in the harbor, the bioluminescence in the water was so incredibly beautiful it was almost frightening. Brilliant little swirls of neon lights all about us in the darkness of the water, like billions of tiny fireflies swimming and playing in wild abandon.

A few days later we reluctantly left the little sanctuary there and cruised on down the lee of the Berry Islands to where we ultimately

115

spent a few days with big black Percy in Little Harbor, trading our American cokes for his delicacies of papaya and sour oranges. And after filling all of our water jugs from Percy's cistern and giving him a box of our .22 cartridges, we headed on around the north side of the Fish Cays and Hall's Spot directly down to Chub Cay. An incredible sail in the lee of the Berrys!

"Take over the helm for a while, will you baby, while I catch a little bit of sleep." I asked Dorothy as we approached Nassau Harbor some nights later. And she beat back and forth outside the entrance until the sun came up so that we could safely enter the harbor on the flood tide.

"Gene!" Dorothy screamed. "Gene! Quick! Help!"

And I lunged up through the companionway just in time to see the ghostly steel hull of a rusty old freighter slip by just a few feet from our bow in the blackness!

Dorothy had jibed to avoid the black monster which had come down on her silently in the gloomy night. And she had back-winded the jib in her confusion and was helplessly without steerage way.

But we had forgotten about it the next morning when we hit the beach in Nassau.

And what a time we had there as we bummed around with the other wayfarers and natives and beachcombers! Like Jack and Wanda Pope aboard their 45 foot ketch as they dove for riches and sunken treasure. And Dale Kelly, the big black fisherman who was always singing the song he had written, *"You Gotta Have Soul if you Vanna'*

116

go to Sea!" And Joe and Bonnie Gallagher aboard their 29 foot Pierson Triton, *"The Bohemian,"* out of Boston. And there were all the curious little shops and native fishing smacks and market places. The reefers and the freighters. The fishing and the rum and the sunshine.

We were 34 days out of Miami when we hoisted main and jenny and reached on out to Rose Island a few miles to the east with the Gallaghers close in our wake.

Dawn the next day saw us running over the hazardous yellow bank from Rose Island directly toward Porgee Rock. But the wind was north northwest ten knots and beautiful, and we almost surfed along wing-in-wing as we eased our course on down more southerly toward Allan's Cays. That night we dropped hook in the anchorage in Highbourne, in the lee of John and Ann Gould's Sally Forth, some two months out of jolly old England. The next day, as we explored the beaches and hills of Highbourne Cay, we learned why Christopher Columbus called these islands, *"The Spice Islands."*

You can smell them!

You can actually smell the spices in the air even when the wind is coming across the open seas. It smells like vanilla and sugar and cinnamon all rolled up, sweet and inviting and tantalizing.

And I was almost free!

A few days later the Gallaghers tried to follow us down to Norman Cay a few miles to the south. But they were afraid to try the hazardous route down through the middle of the Exuma chain and

117

chose to lay to leeward to be safe. But we took the sail right down through the tiny little islands and reefs and coves and bays and lagoons. And it was exciting and beautiful!

That night we broke bread with Robert Manry and his wife and their two teenage kids and German Shepherd dog and cat in their 27 foot Curlew. Bob was the man who gained international fame by sailing his little 12 foot *Tinkerbell* alone across the stormy north Atlantic a year or so earlier.

And then there were Paul and Wanda Sidell of Atlanta, Georgia on their spacious 41 foot Corinthian trimaran Antares.

But the next morning, as I hunted conch from a borrowed dinghy over in the flats, I heard Dorothy scream. And horror pounded at my heart as I saw her dive into the water! I hadn't seen a thing, but I knew one of the children had gone down into the deep!

And neither of the children could swim. But as I watched helplessly from a distance, the owner of the magnificent yacht, *Silver Seas IV*, dove fully clothed off the fly bridge of his ocean-going motor vessel and swam to their aid.

Dorothy was already surfacing with Heather clutched in her grasp by the time he reached them. But she was unable to push Heather up out of the water and back into our boat. And he hoisted them both back aboard the *New Day* before swimming back to his vessel.

A few days later we headed on down the lee of Shroud Cay in the dreamlike Exumas. We were sailing alone this time. Basking in the solitude, Dorothy was lying up on the deck getting a tan all over, and

118

she didn't see the man on the nearby island until he dropped a pile of boards with a loud clatter! And I roared in laughter as she plunged for the companionway.

We were happy!

That night we rafted up with *Windrift* at Hawksbill Cay for a lovely night with another family of "beach bums."

Then on down past Cistern Cay, we finally anchored at dusk about three miles southwest of "haunted" Warderick Cay.

But the next day we almost lost our boat. And our lives!

"Quick, Dorothy! Take the helm! We're almost on that reef!" I shouted as I heaved our biggest Danforth over the side to anchor us against the savage unexpected current that was suddenly washing us over to the breaking reefs on the windward side of Hall's Pond Cay!

The wind had died down and there wasn't enough force in the sails to fight against the incredible tidal current as it raced over the reefs out to the open Atlantic. And we had to lie there at anchor, as the tide gurgled and rushed madly past us, for six hours. The current was so fierce I even had to steer - at anchor - to keep from letting the hull forces pull our anchor up out of the sand below.

But the current finally slacked at the end of the ebb tide, and we ghosted on down past sharks and remoras, visible below us in the clear waters, and around Fowl Cay until we finally threw our lines over the pilings at the Compass Cay dock. As we stepped across the dock, an eight or nine foot black ray slithered silently below our feet in the crystal clear waters.

We replenished our water supply from the rain cistern of the closed Compass Cay Club and bathed and lounged about until Hester Crawford came roaring up in her outboard.

Hester Crawford!

The kind widow of the man who wrote the Air Force song, *"Off We Go Into the Wild Blue Yonder!"* A recluse, philosopher, and expert in unidentified flying objects — she almost always had a glass of some kind in her hand. But she had a lot of love in her heart. And she hosted us there in her lovely little hilltop South Sea island home for a number of days as we swam and snorkeled and hunted for shells and conch.

We were almost free!

I even discovered a cave in one of the tiny nearby offshore islands which no one knew about. Not even Hester. I had followed a giant grouper down down down below the surface to spear him for dinner when he suddenly disappeared under a ledge of the little off-lying island. And as I followed him under the ledge it opened up into a mammoth cave. Big enough to drive a semi-trailer through! It went all the way through the center of the island, clear to the other side. And it was teeming with giant fish — snapper and grouper and parrot fish — bigger than any I had ever seen before!

In those idyllic days we lived on conch and johnny cake—the Bahamian bread — and fish and fruit and rice and wild Bahamian pigeon peas. And the sun and seas and the stars and moon were our companions. The days seemed like paradise. We were kids, romping and playing and having a good time.

Free!

Almost.

But as we sailed on down to Staniel Cay we had to ride out another raging norther in the lee of Big Major's Spot. And then on down past Bitter Guana and Great Guana and Farmers Cays to Galliot Cut where we almost got into trouble again! For as I began to beat into the Cut the waves almost capsized us as the raging ebb tide slammed violently against the strong prevailing southeasterly wind — stacking the seas straight up.

Then on down past Cave and Musha Cays, we headed around Rudder Cut, between Darby Island and Little Darby Island, where we anchored in a lovely and lonely little cove by the beautiful towering white cliffs and the deep emerald green and turquoise waters which crashed into white foam high on the rocks, and ate the fish that night I had caught as we beat down to windward.

Since we didn't have a motor, we had to ghost out of Rudder Cut at slack tide the next day. And then on down past Salt and Lignum Vitae and Adderly and Rat Cays, finally pulling in for the night in the lee of Hog Island.

As usual, by the time we pulled up at the docks, there must have been a couple of dozen smiling black faces with great white teeth and waving hands and a lot of love.

The black Bahamians are beautiful people and they love everybody!

But when I walked up to the little village store and attempted to buy toilet tissue, the people there didn't even know what it was. And there are no Sears Roebuck catalogs or corn cobs on that island! I never have figured that out!

Then on down past Three Sisters Rocks and Rokers Point the next day. But there was no place we could anchor for the night. And another cold front was coming; that meant it was going to be dangerous and rough. So we put out to sea to get away from the foaming reefs and rocks.

All that night we beat back and forth and back and forth, and the next morning with the winds twenty knots out of the south, I bagged the drifter and hoisted the working jib and headed for Conch Cay. We surged on through the entrance to Great Exuma Island as though on a real roller coaster! And then we tacked back and forth on down over the coral heads into Elizabeth Harbor, finally dropping hook in Kidd Cove. Captain Kidd's home! That old pirate!

But the storm was upon us! So we reached across the bay into the lee of Stocking Island where we were in a millpond. There was a sailboat there from Canada and one from Boston. And Toby and Gracie King aboard Pandora out of Annapolis. And there was the fascinating ancient black cargo schooner Anna from Vishy, Australia, whose unbelievably rough and wild-looking crew were much more friendly and hospitable than their countenances foretold.

And then there were the sharks!

We had all been swimming around the boat there in the lee of Stocking Island for several days when one day Dorothy saw a huge shark come up and take a duck that was floating on the surface of the water. And then another shark took another duck: And then another shark another duck. So we didn't swim there anymore!

But it was now the Ides of March and time to head further south. So days later we sailed on down to Man-O-War Cay where we ran back in the lee and anchored for the night. Visions of old Spanish Galleons and pirates and slave traders consumed our imaginations as we gazed up at the remains of the old English fort on the island. For a brief moment, it was as though we were living 400 years ago.

Beating on up to windward the next morning, we made our course on down along Great and Little Exumas inside the reef to the symphony of the sun and great cumulous clouds and a bright blue sky and turquoise waters.

Sailing on down past the little villages of Forbes Hill and Williams Town, we dropped the hook in Hog Cay Cut between Little Exuma and Hog Cay that evening to a bad surge.

We ghosted on out on the flood under Genoa and main the next morning through treacherous shoal waters and reefs.

But the next day — after sailing all night — Nuevitas Light finally showed up on the horizon dead ahead. We were right on course!

As we beat and tacked our way into New Found Harbor, we passed a couple of tiny motorless fishing smacks with white Bahamian natives fishing with hand lines over the reefs in the crystal waters below.

123

That evening, as two of the fishermen sailed their tiny dinghies into our little harbor, we beckoned for them to come over and join us for dinner.

"Hey mon," one of the fishermen exclaimed as he clambered aboard, "you're da only American yacht I've ever seen! And I've fished dese banks all my life!"

"But vat's dis boat made of?" The other one wondered as he ran his hand along the smooth fiberglass gunwales.

"Fiberglass." I answered simply.

"Vat's fiberglass?"

They had never heard of it. And they had never seen the Dacron and nylon that our sails were made of.

We were really getting away from the world.

And at three o'clock the next afternoon, we pulled out of little New Found Harbor under main and jenny — only to discover a little time later that the wind was beginning to gust and gale. But after reefing the main, I set a magnetic course of 143 degrees to Castle Island, but allowed an additional 8 degrees for leeway over the 81 mile course we would have to run across the boisterous seas.

At twilight, with the wind 20 knots and steep and confused seas, Dorothy took the tiller while I tried to rest below in the cold wet cabin.

Later, as the mountainous waves pounded higher and higher in the night and the winds whistled madly through the rigging, I stuck my head up through the companionway in the darkness of the early morning hours to see how Dorothy was doing. And there she was — wet and cold and all wrapped up in her foul weather gear and tied down with her safety lines — huddled over the faint loom of the compass light in the bottom of the cockpit.

"Baby, you shouldn't keep your eyes on the compass like that." I reminded her. "You should look out at the seas and at the sky so that you can keep a steadier course."

"But that way," she shuddered, "I have to look at these waves. And they give me the willies!"

They were huge and threatening and foreboding, particularly in the night, and she didn't even want to look at them as she sat there struggling over the tiller.

So I took over the helm again, and she piled into a pitching bunk below for a little rest. And as the gale howled on and we approached the treacherous Mira Por Vos Shoals, I couldn't help but think of the ominous translation of the frightening Spanish title — "Watch out for yourself!" These shoals had been a sailor's graveyard for hundreds of years.

We were in a main shipping channel and passed a number of freighters in the night — like ghosts with their lights blinking in tantalizing comfort nearby — while we tossed and bobbed and shivered in the cold wet sea. But we were soon tied up to the concrete dock in the lee of Acklin's Island where we were met by a

125

local fisherman who walked us down to the nearest "store" - a 12 x 15 foot room, stocked with only a few bare essentials. But we enjoyed chatting with the proprietor and his wife, and watched as she plucked tiny leaves from a local shrub with which she was going to make home-brewed beer.

After a couple of days relaxing under the lee of China Hill, we finally had to sail for cover under the leeward side of Jamaica Cay as another norther came roaring in off the Atlantic. And roar it did! Day after day! When we finally ran out of drinking water, I rigged up our foul weather gear in the cockpit to funnel the barrage of rain into a bucket. And for several days we lay there hundreds of miles from the nearest real civilization, off to the east of Cuba, while the elements screamed over our little vessel.

But it was time to go back home now.

Little Heather had gotten so lonely without other children that she had invented her own in her imagination. And she would sit there in the cockpit and pretend as though they were there playing with her.

The escape was over.

We weren't really free after all.

And it wasn't nearly as much fun going back. Oh, the islands were still as idyllic and as paradise-like as ever. And the sun and the sea and the stars and the moon were still just as real and as close. Even the clean smell of the sea wind and the taste of the coconut milk and fresh fish were just as wonderful.

126

But it wasn't the same. Because I knew I was going back into that world again. Back into the world from which we had just tried so desperately to flee.

And worse yet, I was no longer a success in that world. I didn't have any money left. My law office was gone. The fancy suits and cars. Our house.

When we finally pulled back up to the dock there in Miami, I was nothing but a penniless beach bum. A vagabond with a doctorate in law, years of trial experience in the criminal courtrooms — and a great big God-shaped hole still in my heart.

So Dorothy and I moved into a humble little house way out on the outskirts of town, and I got a job as a boat carpenter in the prototype shop of the Woodson Boat Company. And nobody knew who I was.

Nobody knew I was a "big shot." One of the leading criminal lawyers in Florida. They thought I was just another sawdust-covered carpenter.

And then I moved to another boat company. And then to another.

And then our marriage finally failed completely.

And Dorothy and I were divorced.

I had really hit the bottom this time!

But I was going to come back. I was going to make it again back to the top.

Back to the very, very top!

9 "WE'RE GONNA NEED SOME MACHINE GUNS!"

"Why don't you come on over here and move in with us?" Harry Susskind phoned me one day. Harry was a wealthy young Jewish bachelor in the wholesale food business, and he and Ed O'Dette, a young bank vice president, shared a big mansion over on Miami Beach that had to be the wildest, swingingest bachelor pad in all South Florida.

There were pet alligators and a raccoon, and piped in stereo in every room, and dimly lit cocktail lounges and sun porches and girls and booze and wild parties.

And so I moved in.

And in a few months I was back practicing law with the firm of Carey Dwyer Austin Cole & Selwood in downtown Miami. And I began making contacts and clawing my way back up to the top again.

Back in *"La Dolce Vita!"* The sweet life.

Make money! And party! That's all there was. I thought.

There was one party at our plush bachelor's "pad" with 400 guests! There was a big band and lots of liquor. We used over 600 pounds of ice cubes in the mixed drinks. And some of the guests brought marijuana and cocaine. And of course there were hoods and lawyers and judges and politicians. And bankers and prostitutes. The party lasted almost three days.

"Man I never saw a party like that in my whole life!" The police sergeant laughed. *"And I've been a cop here on the Beach for twenty years!"* We had hired him to direct the parking and just be around in case we needed him.

But even with all this jet set living I missed Dorothy and the kids. Because I still loved them. And they still loved me.

And so Dorothy and I started dating again. And as lost as we were, we determined to really make a go of it. Nine months later, Judge Ralph Ferguson tied the knot for us a second time. And we started a brand new life.

Lost. But still very much in love.

I soon left the law firm of Carey Dwyer Austin Cole & Selwood to reopen my own criminal law offices downtown.

"I want the largest suite of offices you have." I said to the manager of the Concord Building—right across from the Courthouse on downtown Flagler Street.

"And I want you to knock the wall out between two of the offices and make them into one really big office for me. My investigator will need an office, and my associate will need one. And I'll need space for secretaries, and a reception room and a bar."

The furniture was massive and impressive. My desk was seven or eight feet long. And I set it up with latest and best equipment available - everything including sophisticated eves-dropping devices which enabled me to secretly record conversations in my office. The walnut paneled refrigerator was stocked full of expensive imported champagne and a gigantic hand-carved Mexican breakfront in back of my desk filled with all kinds of liquor.

I was back at the very top!

And I had more business than I could handle. Instead of referring cases out, I would simply set fees so astronomically high that only the richest could afford me. But I guaranteed the results. And so I had to win!

Like the ring of $500-a-night call girls who came to me with a test case one day.

"We'll give you $500 every time you go to court." The expensively dressed and very successful manager of these beautiful ladies explained. "But you gotta guarantee the results. *And we really mean guarantee!*"

But I knew his business was good for at least a grand or so a week to me if I could get the girl off. So I really wanted to win this first case.

"She's gonna do time!" The Miami Beach Vice Squad cop yelled at me. "She and her whole gang are a bunch of filthy little tramps, and they're not doing anything for me! And she kneed me and cursed me when I busted her! *And she's gonna do time! She's goin' away!"*

He was furious!

I had wanted to lay a little bread on him so he'd let her slide on this one. But he wasn't in the market. He was way too mad! And when a cop gets mad enough he won't always take a bribe.

"Fifteen hundred dollars!" the judge said.

To dump the case I had to give the Judge fifteen hundred dollars — and I was only getting five! Which didn't look like very sound mathematics. Unless you considered that by winning this one I'd get a bundle every week out of the ring.

So I did.

And the girl went free. And the Judge got fatter.

Yes, the Miami Beach cops were something else!

And the motorcycle cops are unreal!

There's one traffic intersection on the Beach where five streets come together at one place. Right where all the wealthy snowbird tourists have to drive their big Lincolns and Caddy's and Mercedes. And there's just no way you can get through that intersection during the busy tourist season without violating some little minor section of the Traffic Code. Which makes it a gold mine for the brazen traffic cops.

132

"O.K. sister. Lemme see your license!" The routine goes. "You failed to yield the right-of-way back there at that intersection. So you gotta go to court. Ninety days from now."

"But officer," the little old lady explains through her mink and diamonds, "I'll be back in New Jersey then!"

"Well, okay. Get outa' the car! I'll have to take you in!"

"*Oh no! Officer,* please! Can't I just pay *you*? And then you pay the fine for me? *Please!*"

"Well . . . okay. I guess so. . . ."

And so he pulls in an extra couple of hundred a day.

The spot is so good the motorcycle officers line up in a row down the little hidden alley. Waiting their turn to pick off the sitting duck tourist.

But then here comes Jimmy Nasella one day. Remember Jimmy? The feisty little criminal lawyer from the Public Defender's Office? Jimmy had lived on the Beach forty years and knew every cop and hooker and bookie and bartender on the strip.

And along he came one day, right through that intersection in rush hour traffic. At about 85 miles an hour! And dead drunk!

"*Rrrrrrrrrrrrrrr!*" The motorcycle siren screamed after him.

133

"Oh, it's you Jimmy! Damn you! Now just look what you've gone and done! You made me lose my place in line! Damn it, Jimmy! Now get outa here and go sleep it off. And slow down - will you?"

And Augie Iverlieno knew the Beach cops pretty well too. Augie was a booster client of mine who got busted one day on about 75 bench warrants for traffic and parking violations. But he wasn't worried about a few dozen traffic tickets because he was making fifty or seventy-five thousand a year just off of the men's suits he boosted out of department stores around South Florida.

"Augie, I've got to take you in." The Miami Beach police officer apologized. Augie was a big man on the Beach. "I hate to, but I just gotta. Now you've gotta come with me, Augie, please!"

"Yeah. Well... all right. I'll go with you." Augie finally relented. "But only if you get Gene Neill for me, and only if you'll drop me by my apartment first so I can pick up a little grass on the way in."

So the cop took him by his apartment, and Augie got some marijuana to take to jail with him and keep himself in good spirits until I got him out. And incidentally — his 75 bench warrants only cost him a $20 fine because the judge was a drinking pal of mine. And we "tried" all the cases in his chambers.

By the time I was forty I had everything you can buy with money. I had had one airplane and was getting ready to buy another. A big house in suburbia. A brand new Mercedez Benz and an expensive custom sports car the Ford Motor Company had built as a show car and taken all around the States. I had motorcycles and sailboats, and

134

I belonged to all the groovy little private "key clubs" and racquet clubs and such all over South Florida.

Big time hoods started hanging around my office and drinking my champagne — and doing all kinds of things.

And I had a couple of gorillas who worked for me too. Big John and Blackie. I paid them to do my strong arm errands for me. Collect money. Talk people into things. Or talk people out of things.

Irv Weinstein was my investigator. A super-sharp red-headed Jew who knew every cop and bondsman and thief and prostitute south of Jacksonville. Each one of them owed him a favor. And I collected on every one of them.

And the bondsmen and the cops hustled cases to me. Word was out in the underworld, *"If you want off - get Gene Neill."*

Even the downtown police hung out in my office. I had given them all keys so they could come up in the evenings and on weekends with their girlfriends or hood friends and booze it up or transact business or play games. Whatever they wanted.

And I always carried a .45 Colt Commander with a custom action and loaded with big Erma hollow points.

Although I never had to shoot anyone, I came awfully close several times.

Like when the big Chicago car theft ring sent the gorilla down to try and muscle me into giving them back a hot Cadillac Eldorado. A banker client of mine had bought it from them, and now they were going to try and steal it back—or scare him out of it. A favorite underworld trick. But the goon they sent wasn't bright enough to figure on a lawyer with a .45 full of dum dums. And when I pointed that man-hole sized barrel between his eyes there in the swank Miami Beach hotel and ordered him to take his clothes off, he got humble awfully fast.

Funny how insecure you get when you're standing half-naked — looking into a cannon like that.

But I also carried a switchblade knife and I used it, too.

Like the time outside the Twenty-Seven Birds Lounge down in Coconut Grove. In the black early morning hours.

"Bam!" The big guy smashed my face with his sledge hammer fist.

And as a linebacker for the Dallas Cowboys professional football team, Paul Jones really packed a wallop.

I had just been standing there with my hands in my pockets "minding my own business." Oh, I had thrown some wise cracks at him in the bar. I was bad about that. I was a mean drunk.

But my big drunk 6'2" and 235 pounds only swayed an inch or so under his heavy blow.

"Is that the best punch you've got little man!" I mocked him. But my mind was racing.

136

I knew he wasn't a dynamite boxer or street fighter, or he wouldn't have led with his right. And he wouldn't have just smashed me on my cheekbone. He would have hit my mouth or nose with a left jab and then followed through with his right. And I'd have been done.

But I also knew he was a professional athlete in top physical shape; and if I started trading punches with him, he'd eventually pound me into the ground.

"Bam!" He smashed me harder this time, 'cause now he was really mad!

And people were beginning to gather around. Including Buck Virgel my old lawyer pal.

"Not very strong are you, little fella," I dug into his craw again. But as I said it my fingers closed around the switchblade knife in my right pocket and my thumb found the button.

"Bam!" His huge fist smashed home a third time.

But my knife slashed out at the same instant, and his blood spattered my car! And then I really got brave and started chasing him. Across 27th Avenue, down Aviation Avenue, all the way to South Bayshore Drive. But a lawyer in leather-soled Florsheim Imperials can't catch a football player who's running from a knife.

What an unbelievable life!

And back in my law office, under the cushion of my chair, I had a pistol with a silence. And machine guns and plastic explosives and stolen drivers' licenses and passports and drugs were usually hidden away around the offices.

Most of my clients were in the drug business, and some of them would pay off their fees in cocaine or heroin or hashish. So there was always some of it around. And I would offer my underworld clients a couple of lines of coke just like some lawyers would offer a cigarette.

"My God, Gene, you've lost control of your life!" Jim Miller, a lawyer friend of mine frowned at me incredulously one day in my office as he gradually began to comprehend what kind of operation I was running. "Don't you *know* you're gonna fall! *You can't keep going like this!"*

But I just laughed at him. I thought I was invincible. Invisible.

Even when we used to shoot the machine guns just for kicks.

"Hey, it's my turn!" Sgt. Willie Chippas of the City of Miami Police Department laughed one day as he grabbed the nine millimeter Schmeizer submachine gun out of the other officer's hand.

"VRRROOOOMMMM!" The machine gun belched as he ripped off a half a clip of copper-jacketed parabellums into a big stack of old file folders and cardboard boxes.

"BOM BOM BOM!!" The slower firing English Sten answered from the hands of the other cop as he poured back some more lead into the same stack of old files.

138

And I guess we must have run thousands of shells through the pistol with the silencer as I showed it off to people who had never seen a professional killer's gun. And that's what this one was. Because it had been used by a little Italian in a dark parking lot one night. A little Italian client of mine.

It was a dream world of crime and booze and violence. Of getting criminals off. Getting their cases fixed. Living with them. Playing with them.

But there were lighter moments too. Like the time I was waiting there in my office with little Tony Fusco and his wife out of Fort Lauderdale. Waiting to go to Court where I already had a deal on his counterfeiting case.

But little Tony was still nervous and scared and shaking. He had a long rap sheet, and he knew that if he took another fall he was going away for a long time. So he was chain-smoking as he paced up and down my suite looking for reassurance. And glancing at his watch every few seconds.

I always kept a little nickel-plated .22 magnum Derringer on the marble pen stand in the center front of my desk. And it looked just like a little toy. But those .22 magnum hollow points will make a bigger hole than a .38 Special in a ballistics gelatin test. Or in a man. And as nervous little Tony started to light up his hundredth cigarette for the afternoon he saw the Derringer and thought it was one of those cute little pistol cigarette lighters.

And he picked it up and pulled the trigger! Right by the end of his cigarette.

"BBAAAAMMMMMM!" The magnum splintered through the wall a few feet from my right shoulder!

I thought he was going to have a coronary!

But shaking like a leaf, he went free later that afternoon.

And then another time Willie Chippas, the downtown police sergeant, was playing with a pistol in my office when it went off from the half-cocked position, accidentally ripping a .45 hollow point through the wall.

And of course, I lived in the cocktail lounges where the gangsters hung out. The Racquet Club, The Admiral "V" and the Penguin Club. All the little private joints over on the Beach and on the Causeway around the Place for Steaks. Wherever the big-time hoods were doing their thing. And I had lunch many days with Norman Rothman and some of his pals.

And they liked me. I was one of them, and I got results. They trusted me. And they came to me.

I was right on top in the criminal law field.

But I was miserable! And many nights I would silently cry myself to sleep.

Life was senseless and psychotic and worthless. And I wanted to die.

Because there was no other way out.

So for excitement I suppose, and possibly for the money — or maybe just because I was looking for something to fill that hole in my life — I started getting involved deeper in crime.

"Gene, we can take my company for a great big bundle if you'll help me with my paperwork." Bob Bennett whispered over a cocktail in my office one day.

Bob was an executive with Continental National American Group. And a swinging bachelor who hung around my offices all the time.

And so we took his company. We set up phony automobile accidents with phony doctors and medical reports and police reports. Bob had the authority to sign checks, so he settled each make-believe case by simply bringing his checkbook over and making out a big check to the make-believe lawyers. Then we would forge endorsements on the checks and run them through phony accounts.

Perfect crimes.

And a lot of my clients were involved in cocaine in a big way. It's a lot better business than heroin. I even flew down with them to Bogotá, Columbia—the cocaine capitol of the world—and showed them how to get cocaine into the country. It was easy if you knew how. And we were in the process of setting up a cocaine processing plant on the outskirts of Bogotá. We had a young chemist down there from Miami who was going to run the show on that end.

"Yeah." He bragged. "My lawyer lost the trial. So while I was out on supersedeas bond pending appeal from my conviction, I drove my car down to Miami Beach. I just left a suicide note in the car and walked out into the surf. Then I trudged down through the water a few hundred yards, and came back up to the beach and split out of the country. I like Bogotá, so I'm just gonna stay down here. And if you can take care of the cocaine after I synthesize it — we'll have a real good thing going! We can make a billion dollars!"

I had met with him in the Hotel Tekendama in Bogotá along with some other cocaine manufacturers and exporters there. And we were going to make the cocaine right. Instead of using kerosene or gasoline to boil off the paste, we were going to use ether. Ours would be the finest quality in the world.

And then there was the bank robbery.

Down on the southern end of Florida there's a chain of islands called the Florida Keys. They stretch all the way from the southern tip of Florida down to Key West about ninety miles away. A tiny island and a bridge. And then another island and another bridge. On and on.

And on one of these islands was a big fat Federal Bank. The nearest "fuzz" was a little jerkwater police station about thirty miles to the north.

There just weren't any other cops around.

"Now here's the way to do it!" I began explaining to the little Italian sitting across from my desk.

"Here's the island here on this map. Just blow up the bridge here on the north side of the island, and blow up the bridge here on the south side of the island. And at the same time, by-pass the ADT system. And then you can just walk in the bank and wipe it out. All the time you need! And then you can leave in a stolen speedboat which will be waiting right here. Run it in back of this island here, sink the boat with a hand grenade, and take off in the amphibious helicopter which will be waiting for you. We already have the pilot."

"They won't know what hit them. Or how you got there. Or how you got away."

"It'll be perfect!"

They were all "perfect crimes." No way I could get caught.

And so it went. And I got deeper and deeper.

But it was only a matter of time.

10   THE NOOSE TIGHTENS

Big old burly Henry Rolle was from the Cayman Islands. A lazy, quiet, faraway little handful of paradise down off the south coast of Cuba. An idyllic little world all to itself, tucked away in the warm and basking Caribbean.

A perfect place to go get away from it all.

But also a perfect place for smuggling cocaine.

And that was old Henry's bag. And he was good at it, because his tiny fleet of little reefers and cargo vessels made a perfect front for getting the cocaine out of Bogotá and into Miami. Through the Caribbean Islands.

And he brought in millions of dollars' worth.

But he made the mistake that trips up almost every criminal. He trusted someone.

The same mistake I made.

"Shazam!" Little Captain Marvel was now suddenly the big man on campus!

And I threw myself into building racing engines and cars with an absolute frenzy.

"The Yokosuka Raiders!" they used to call us. And like Marines everywhere we tore the town apart.

But with a huff and a snort and an upturned nose the chef finally relented by not too politely placing a glass of milk in front of Dorothy. And our wedding was complete.

Round and round and round. The *"Devil's Triangle"*!

My first day in the free world!

Heading for California! Like the "Grapes of Wrath"!

Red Square. Moscow, Russia! **Got arrested three times in three months! (Bible in hand).**

The KGB thought the CIA had sent me.

...but the Russian Christians loved me!

Three months in Russia will plum wear you out!

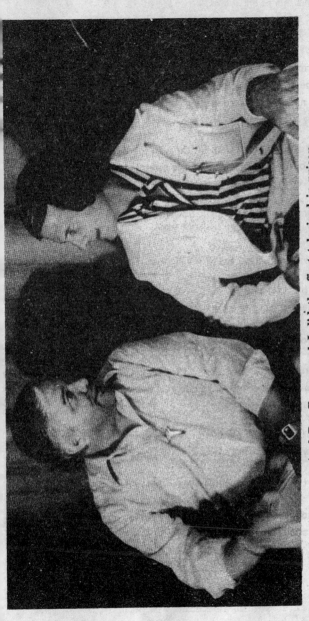

And Pat Boone and I did the first televised in-prison revival in history.

He told them about the big load that he was going to bring in through a motel in Hialeah, Florida, and his friend set him up with the narcs. They were waiting for him there in the darkness, in the early morning hours.

And as he stepped from his car with the big eight kilo polyethylene bag of uncut cocaine, the police swarmed out of the shadows with guns drawn.

They had him dead! Right down to his fingerprints on the bag. *A perfect case!*

He was going to go away for a lifetime.

But he bonded out and came to see me. And before he even spoke to me, he first came to court and watched me try several cases just to see what I could do. He had gotten the word I was the one to get him off, but he wanted to see me in action.

"All right, Mr. Lawyer mahn." His Cayman voice lilted. "I've seen you in da court, and indeed you do vell. But can you get me off? And if so, how much vill it cost?"

"Yes I can get you off. But it won't be easy. And it's going to cost you everything you have."

And I set a fee that would boggle most men's minds. But I knew he was scared. Under that calm poker face and deceptively tranquil island facade he was terrified inside! In fact I never saw a man who was as afraid of iron bars.

158

So he gave me a big bundle of money.

And I had a little chat with the prosecutor. And the case was never even filed! A perfect case for the State, but Rolle never even had to go to court!

"All right, Henry, you're a free man now. And you can forget about the whole thing. But what about the rest of my money?"

"But mahn, I just haven't got it." He squirmed. Because he had seen the fellows who did my "collection work."

"But I still have three more kilos of coke! And I'll give dat to you instead of da money, if you'll take it. And it's vorth a lot more dahn vhat I owe you."

"All right, I'll take it. Where is it?"

"Veil, dere's a problem dere." He chuckled. "I've given it to Mario to sell for me on consignment. And he von't vant to give it back."

And indeed he didn't. Mario would kill for 500 bucks. And he wasn't about to turn loose of all that coke.

So two of my men had to go take it from him. At gunpoint. In front of his wife and kids and next door neighbors. In fact, they held them all captive at gunpoint while Mario went out to get the cocaine from where it was stashed.

And there it was on my desk — a half a million dollars' worth of dreams. Shining up at me like 6.6 pounds of sparkling sugar crystals.

159

That night I hid it up above the acoustical tile outside my office by the elevator in the hall. Where no one would find it. And where if they did find it, they wouldn't be able to pin it on me.

Oh I was so smart. I thought.

And I started looking for a buyer.

And along came my good friend Jim Stanfill.

Good old Jim! I'd gotten him out of jail three or four times. I'd kept him from going to prison for years. He owed me his life.

Jim was sharp and ambitious and ruthless. He knew every cop and hood and junkie on the east coast. And he was into all kinds of things.

"Who's in town that can handle three kilos of coke real fast and safely and neatly for me, Jim?" I asked him one day in my office as I pitched him a sample matchbox full of it across my desk.

"Hey yeah — I know just the guy!" He grinned as he rubbed some of it on his gums and touched it to the end of his tongue and burned a little on tin foil to check it out. "He's a big buyer from New York. And he's here in town. He has a whole trunk full of money! I've seen it. I'll get him and bring him over if you'll give me ten percent of the action."

"Go get him!"

And he did.

160

I had trusted Jim.

And when I met this buyer downstairs in Sally Russell's cocktail lounge, I knew he was no cop. A handsome 60 years, well-manicured. Hair of silver. Eyes like cold steel. He had on expensive tailored English threads and handmade Italian shoes. And he really knew his business.

"Tell me about the markets in Algeria and Turkey." I questioned him to see how much he knew. "And what about Kowloon and Portugal?"

And he had all the right answers. He knew the world market inside out like only a real top notch buyer would.

"Casey." He called himself.

We both laughed when I asked him for his I.D. because it, of course, was phony. But it was well done. Really professional.

So I went back to my office and sent him a sample by Jim Stanfill and told him to give me a price.

And the next day Stanfill came back with a price. Low — but okay for openers. Particularly considering I had cut the stuff to pay off thee gorillas who had taken it from Mario.

So when Casey showed up at my office the next day, he had a briefcase full of fifty dollar bills.

But just to make doubly certain, I scanned him electronically before I began talking to him. I had a device that would pick up any kind of eavesdropping equipment which might be secreted on him. It sent an electronic beam toward him, and as I dialed all the available frequencies on the scanner, that beam would bounce back audibly and show on a meter if he was bugged.

But he was clean.

And I had sent everybody out of the office. We were alone. The front door was locked, and there was no way some of his pals could come in and rip off the cocaine. Or my money. Or both.

So he gave me the money, and I locked it away and ushered him toward the door.

"Come on, I'll get the stuff." I told him.

"Where is it?" He asked as we approached the elevator apparently to leave the building.

"Right straight above your head in that acoustical tile." I grinned.

"That's good! That's smart!" He smiled for the first time as we slid a chair over for him to get his purchase down.

And as I walked him down Flagler Street to put him in a cab, the tension was easing. The deal was over and clean.

But then here came the cop!

162

"Hold it there, Neill!" The uniformed police officer shouted angrily from across the street as he put his hand on the butt of his low slung service revolver!

But Casey never lost his cool at all. His steel eyes just flicked over to mine piercingly. Inquiringly. Demandingly.

"Don't worry about it." I tried to smile. "He's just a friend of mine playing games." And I put my hand inside my coat to the cold butt of my .45 automatic—a gesture my cop friend well knew. And the cop finally broke into a grin.

"Beat ya to the draw again, huh, mouthpiece?"

"Yeah, but get lost! I'll see you in a minute!" I threw back at him as I hustled Casey into a cab and off to New York with his cocaine.

"You dumb flatfoot!" I pretended to be angry at my police officer friend. "The briefcase that guy was carrying was full of three kilos of coke I just sold him! And you almost queered the deal! You're lucky he didn't blow you away!"

"Well hey! Gee I'm sorry!" He apologized sarcastically. "I sure wouldn't have wanted to have interfered with your business! After all, you poor lawyers have got to make a living!"

That's how well I knew the cop. He knew that I was serious about the cocaine. But he didn't care. He only wished that he had been in on the action. And he knew that if he hung around me long enough, maybe he might be in on the next one.

163

In fact I would park my Mercedes right square in front of the entrance to my building in the *"No Parking - Tow Away Zone."* And every morning the cop would come by and put a ticket on the windshield. But he would make very sure that he wrote the wrong license number on the ticket. So when I would get in the car to drive off, I would just tear up the ticket. And when the bench warrant was issued, it was issued against some non-existent license plate. Or against somebody else's license plate.

And I got free parking. Right at my front door.

Police protection.

All down the line. From parking tickets to bank robberies.

But later I was to learn who Casey really was. He wasn't a big syndicate buyer from New York.

He was a special undercover agent of the United States government who had been flown in from England just to come over and buy my cocaine!

When my trusted old pal Jim Stanfill had left my office that day to go get his buyer "friend" — the one whom he said he had seen with the trunk full of money —*he had gone straight to the police.*

He went to detective Ray Havens of the Organized Crime Division of the Dade County Public Safety Department and told him the whole story. He had even told Havens I could do a *hundred pounds of coke a day* because he thought I already had my plant in operation down in Bogotá.

Needless to say, the police did some real nice things for my friend Jim. But that's the way the game goes.

But the reason they had sent all the way to England for this "Casey" was because they knew I knew too many cops. And they knew it was going to take a real bright one to fool me.

And Casey did.

They had really picked a winner!

Mighty Casey struck me out.

And after I sold him the cocaine he started calling me on the phone. At the office and at home — all hours of the day and night. Trying to buy more. And asking me questions every once in a while about some of my contacts.

I began to smell a rat because this didn't fit with the rest of Casey's cool. Real buyers just never use a telephone. And they never ask questions. Cause that's a good way to wind up dead.

But Casey knew he had all he was ever going to get on me now. So he could afford to start getting careless. Start reaching way out.

And I could feel the noose tightening on my neck. And I began seeing cars following me from time to time. And I got cold all over.

And I knew the end was near.

The end of my life.

11   THE LAST CHANCE

And that's where I was.

So I drove my Mercedes down to Honda Miami, a big motorcycle dealer, with a big wad of some of the fifty dollar bills Casey had given me for the cocaine.

"I'll take that big red Honda 750 over there." I said to the owner. And I'll take a set of saddle bags and a couple of helmets. I want you to really check the bike over carefully because I want to take a long trip on it, and I want it to be perfect."

And after I had broken it in for a couple of weeks, I took it back up to the shop and had them crate it for me and ship it by Air Express from Miami to San Jose, Costa Rica.

I got my associate, Ray Gist, to take over my practice while I was gone. And after I flushed about a half a pound of cocaine which I had hidden down the toilet, Dorothy and I caught a jet airliner to San Jose, Costa Rica.

I was going to find us a faraway place somewhere.

A hiding place.

And as I gazed out of the window of our plane as we came in low over the jungles and swamps and winding rivers of eastern Costa Rica, I longed to be down there in a canoe. Away from it all. Living in a little hut, maybe. Long ago memories of jungle cathedrals and orchids and wild otters slipped back into view for the first time in many years.

I was looking for one more chance.

And as we let down into San Jose, below the two towering peaks of the majestic volcanoes *Irazu and Turrialba,* I thought maybe I could find a little mountain village someplace, where we could buy a parcel of land, and live happily forever after. And suddenly I got just a tiny glimpse of that new chance. A feeling that maybe there was someplace where we could get away. Maybe there was a jungle stream somewhere. Or a lake. Maybe there still was someplace!

But this was my last chance!

But then I had always been dreaming.

And as Russell Bartmus, my old hood pal from Miami, met us as we disembarked the airplane, it quickly brought me back out of my dream. Russell was an incredible man! He had been a graduate of

Annapolis Naval Academy. A strong, handsome weightlifter in his forties. He had been all over the world. Done all kinds of things.

But Russ was a terrible man back then. Really lost.

He had put his .38 snub-nosed revolver against a girl's head in his car one night in Miami and forced her to do all kinds of things. And when I got him off, he left the country and went down to San Jose to open a brothel. Prostitution is legal there, and he bought a wild honky tonk little bar there called the "Tio Sam." Out of which he operated his filthy trade.

But the last time I saw Russ he was a changed man. A Christian in a prison ministry.

But Dorothy couldn't stand Russ back then. And so we didn't see much of him those few days there in San Jose while we were waiting for our motorcycle to clear customs. We just walked around town from our Hotel Chorotega Tower and played tourist. And a couple of days later they fork-lifted our crated bike out onto the asphalt strip beside the customs warehouse where we eagerly uncrated it.

I guess there must have been twenty fascinated Costa Ricans who wanted to try to help the crazy gringos get their big four cylinder motorcycle out of its cage.

In fact one of our "helpers" wanted to use the crate for a chicken coop. And I suppose he did.

After riding the bike back to our hotel to pack all of our goods into the saddlebags, we roared off down Central Avenue and Paseo

Colon and the Auto Pista heading north. We must have looked like something from Mars to those Costa Ricans! We were dressed in custom-tailored white leather riding outfits with full white Bell helmets, and astride that monstrous metallic red four-banger! We roared along like nothing they had ever seen before.

Up into the wilds of the Cardillera de Tilaran Mountains. Then down the snake-like turns to the Pacific at Puntarenas.

"You must be from the Mafia!" Miguel Gomez laughed in almost perfect English when I told him I was a criminal lawyer from Miami. He was the owner of the Hotel Tioga where we stayed that evening.

But his joke wasn't very funny to me.

Then on back up into the mountains the next morning, we crossed over from Costa Rica into Nicaragua—with a whole lot of hassle at the border.

Then on past Lago de Nicaragua, the only fresh water lake in the world where sharks and swordfish abound!

I was beginning to feel free again. And every time I saw a little village or an island or a mountain or a road leading up into the clouds, I would say to myself, "Is this it? Is this the place for me to turn and go find the little farm for us? The little rancho?"

We made notes of each of the spots that particularly appealed to us so that when we got back home we could pick out the one place that was meant for us and come back and buy it.

170

"Honey! Just look at that castle!" Dorothy exclaimed. And sure enough, atop a small mountain by Lake Masaya on our left was a real medieval castle perched majestically on the cliff overlooking the water below. One of those places where you can drift off like in a time machine — back through the centuries.

"Maybe that little cliff across the lake from the castle is the place for us!" I shot back at her seriously.

But we barreled on down past Lake Tipitapa, with its incredible boneless fish, and on up into the steep Cordillera Horno Grande Mountains. And then across the border and into Honduras.

"What's that man doing with that spray gun?'" Dorothy frowned at me quizzically as she watched the little man diligently and carefully spraying our motorcycle with an aerosol spray can.

"Fumigating our bike! What else?" I joked.

And he was. Fumigating our bike!

But then back down from the majestic and cool heights to the hot humid lowlands, we sped on over the rolling open range cattle country of Honduras and into El Salvador.

Where we promptly got lost.

But we found one of the most beautiful little towns I've ever seen in the world. San Miguel, El Salvador. With its shuddering and omnipresent volcano.

171

And I thought maybe this was it! With its magnificent cathedral and city square and benches and flowers and lovely people. A little wonderland hidden away from the world. Off the beaten path where no one would ever find us or bother us.

But as I went into the bank to exchange some currency, I was quickly reminded that this was really a frontier town.

Pistols everywhere!

All the well-dressed and courteous young male bank tellers wore very business-like .38's strapped at their waists. And the very helpful doorman had a Thompson .45 caliber machine gun slung over his shoulder to keep company with the revolver in his belt!

We were really out on the edge of civilization.

But in most of the cities in El Salvador the police didn't carry guns. Instead they had long two-foot, nickel- plated, brass-knuckled machetes hanging at their sides! In shiny black leather scabbards. With lots of nickel-plated rivets and white tassels and bobbles and bangles. And they looked as though they wouldn't hesitate to use them for a second if they thought they had to!

"The Savior of the World!" Proclaimed the mammoth and extraordinarily impressive monument — to a man named Jesus — there in the capitol.

I can recall glancing at it as we rode past. *"Jesus."* I remember passively thinking. "I wonder who he really was."

172

Little did I know then that I was going to meet Him one day very soon. Standing in the shadows of a little solitary cell in a maximum security Federal prison. While I was serving a fifty-year prison sentence!

But we motored on up through the mountains a couple more days to the border into Guatemala. *Only nobody warned us that they had orders there to shoot us on sight!*

"Baby, they're pointing those machine guns at US!" I yelled back at Dorothy as we roared up the road.

And sure enough they were!

From the huge elevated poured concrete machine gun turrets lining both sides of the highway there near the border.

And I could just see the faces in back of the machine guns. And they weren't smiling! It didn't take too much smarts to figure out something was wrong. But I smiled and waved and tried to appear like a dumb happy tourist. *Much in love with the local natives!*

But I noticed their machine guns followed us the entire way until we were over the hill safely out of their range.

Whew!

And *then* they told us!

When we pulled in for breakfast at the super-clean little restaurant in Jutiapa, we pieced together in our broken Spanish the explanation from the courteous old restaurant owner.

"Guatemala City has been under siege for months by guerillas up in the mountains." He pointed up into the hills.

"Every day the guerillas come roaring down out of the mountains on motorcycles with two men on each motorcycle. And the man on back always has a machine gun. They shoot up the town and the soldiers and rob the bank. And then they roar back up into their mountain hideouts before the militiamen can catch them!"

"And so," he concluded gravely, "the President has made it a law that two people are not allowed to ride on a motorcycle at one time. *And they may shoot you if they see the two of you on the motorcycle!*"

"Great!" I turned to Dorothy.

"Yeah! Isn't that just dandy!" She replied.

"Here we are on the southern border of Guatemala," I mused, "and we've got to drive all the way through to Mexico. And if anybody sees us riding together they'll shoot us!"

But we didn't have much choice, so we just decided to do the best we could. And after breakfast, we headed on up into the cold mountains around the side of Suchitan Volcano. But I made sure Dorothy left her helmet off so the soldiers would see her long red hair.

174

"Guerillas," I figured, "don't have long red hair."

And as we came around a cold mountain curve — there lay Guatemala City in the valley below! Majestic and impressive!

But at the very first comer a little man with a very big Thompson .45 caliber machine gun pulled us over and chewed us out thoroughly in Spanish. But we played dumb and left pretending that we thought that he was giving us some directions. As we pulled away from him — still riding double — I listened very carefully to see if I could hear him slide the bolt back on that Tommy. And then, of all things, we had to drive all around town trying to find the Mexican Consulate so that we could get visas into Mexico.

We finally got our visas, and started again across town — still riding double. But we got stopped at every corner.

The first few times, I simply told Dorothy to go ahead and walk around the next corner. And then I would come around there and pick her up as soon as we were out of sight of the gunmen. But after a few blocks of this we gave up, and I put her in a taxicab and asked him to drive her across town as I followed behind on the bike.

Away at last from the militiamen and their machine guns, we mounted back up double and headed on up into the cold misty mountains to one of the most beautiful cities in the Western Hemisphere.

Antigua, Guatemala!

We checked into the absolutely lovely Hotel Antigua where our private little cottage overlooked a garden aflame with flowers and colorful macaws and lovely trees.

The next morning after breakfast, I called my associate Ray Glist back in Miami to see how the law practice was going.

"Everything is just great!" Ray encouraged me. "Stay there as long as you want and I'll mail you a check once a month!"

He didn't know I was really thinking of staying there.

In Guatemala Dorothy and I both found a country we really liked. A country where we would gladly spend the rest of our lives. A country full of lovely people.

But we wanted to see the rest of it, so the next day we were off to incredible Lake Atitlan. The 22 kilometers to Chimaltenango were filled with beautiful pine woods and rolling plush green grass, sheep and little mountain streams, and quaint little ancient Spanish bridges. There were hanging bird nests and Gila monsters, caracaras and giant frogs, hummingbirds and parrots.

The kind of place you'd like to just pull over to the side of the road and say, "Well, this is it! I'm going to just stay right here!"

But then on west to Patzicia. And from there on—Wow!

Straight up and straight down! The well-paved but narrow little highway was more vertical than it was horizontal. The sixteen kilometers from Patzicia to Lake Atitlan were the steepest and most mountainous I had ever seen.

And the most marvelous!

I had to use low gear for mile after mile climbing uphill. And then coming down the other side, even if I left the bike in low gear, the roads were so steep that I had to also use the brakes to keep from accelerating too rapidly. The altitude must have been ten to fourteen thousand feet, and the temperature was in the forties. In fact I finally had to pull off the road and put a hotter set of plugs in our engine to compensate for the lack of oxygen in those high altitudes.

Lake Atitlan!

Just like a dream with those huge towering volcanoes on the other side of the lake. Beautiful. Peaceful. Idyllic.

But then we got arrested!

By a little man with a great big machine gun.

Another little man with a great big Thompson submachine gun— who made us walk in front of him all the way to the police station.

"Right now!" As he so succinctly put it in Spanish.

And there was the big old fat Jefe! With a big fat cigar in his mouth and a big fat smile on his face. Just the kind of big fat jovial man you'd expect to be the Chief of Police of a lovely mountaintop village in Guatemala. And when I convinced him that we were just dumb Yankee tourists, he smiled and gave us a *"Buen suerta"* - *"good luck"* - and sent us on our merry way.

In just a few more kilometers we came back onto the Pan American Highway. And then another turnoff to the north to inimitable Chichicastenango!

Where I got the chief witch doctor drunk.

He really runs the town; and although he didn't come right out and say it, he apparently offers animal sacrifices up on the mountain near the town.

But he sure does like fire water!

A few days later we roared on up through the very cold Sierra Madre mountain range past one landslide after another. And past flocks of multi-colored parrots and tropical birds and dense trees, on into Mexico. And a driving rain!

"I wonder what those kids are picking up out there?" I thought to myself as I sat at the breakfast table the next morning, waiting as Dorothy showered and did whatever it is women do each morning that always seems to take so long.

The little boys were gleefully picking something up out of the gutters and off of the cars and sidewalks and streets, and putting them in little containers. Like kids on an Easter egg hunt.

178

I found out later what they were gathering, because they came around with a great big bowl of these things after their mother had fried them, and offered me some to eat.

Beetles!

"No thanks fellas! I appreciate it. But no thanks!" I smiled at them in my limited Spanish, as my stomach turned flip-flops at the sight of the bowl of greasy little black bugs.

And then on down the west side of the Sierra Madres to Juchitan — where Dorothy almost got us arrested again!

"Give me your passports!" the big fat army officer growled at us after he had flagged us off to the side of the road. But you can growl if you have a big fat .45 on your hip like he did.

"Our passports?" Dorothy practically shouted at him as her red-headed temper flashed. She wasn't about to let any big fat Mexican soldier push her around — with or without a .45.

"Cool it there, baby!" I whispered in her ear as I pushed her aside to hand the now glaring official our passports. And I laid a few pleasant platitudes on him in Spanish in order to simmer down the impending international incident. And after his ego was sufficiently reestablished, he allowed us somewhat grudgingly to go on our way.

On through the Sierra Madres to Oaxaca, with its Mayan ruins and medieval basilicas and churches and monuments.

Then up through more fantastic mountains the next morning — through mile after mile of thrilling vistas — into Mexico City in a deluge of rain.

But we already knew Mexico City pretty well. Because back while I was in the Public Defender's Office we rode a different Honda motorcycle all the way from Miami to Mexico City, and then back to Miami. In fact, a feature article was published about the trip in the June 1966 issue of Cycle World Magazine.

Anyway, after a few days in that big old dirty city, we sped on up into the Sierra Madres again—250 kilometers of going straight up and straight down for the next few days. Incredible and indescribable mountain roads with virtually no traffic at all.

And no gas stations.

On one occasion we even bought gas out of a 55 gallon drum in the back room of a little grocery store on the side of the highway!

But finally we crossed back into Texas.

And that night in our motel room we began to plan our next move.

"Honey, what about Guatemala?" I asked Dorothy that evening.

"Why don't you fly back down there after we've gotten back to Miami and see if you can find us a place to live? Maybe in Antigua or that beautiful little nine kilometer stretch of paradise between the highway and Antigua."

"Sounds great to me!" Dorothy agreed. She was as ready to get out of the rat race as I was.

But we didn't know what was waiting back in Miami!

Police. With guns. And warrants for my arrest.

So we headed on up through Corpus Christi and San Jacinto and Beaumont into Lafayette, Louisiana that night. And the next couple of days the big old deep shade of the ancient Spanish moss-draped oaks kept us from the blazing summer sun as we passed Morgan city and crossed the mighty muddy Mississippi. Then across Lake Ponchatrain and Bay Saint Louis through the carnival and striptease joint atmosphere of Gulf Port and Biloxi, Mississippi.

Then Fort Walton Beach, Florida!

The same Fort Walton Beach where the Eglin Air Force Base is located. And the Eglin Air Force Base is where the Federal Prison Camp is located.

The Federal Prison Camp where I was to wind up doing time very soon!

But of course I never gave it a thought then.

And twenty-four days — and 6,421 miles later—we were back at our house, 6950 S. W. 98th Street. South Miami, Florida.

A fantastic trip through six foreign countries and five states. As far as across America and back again.

And the world was almost behind us; criminal law was almost behind us.

All I had to do was tie up a few loose ends at the office and then we'd go live happily forever after.

But the police were waiting for me!

The Federal Grand Jury had already handed down a secret sealed indictment. And the Federal Government was ready to arrest me.

The end had come.

It had finally come.

12   "GET UP AGAINST THE WALL!"

When I hit my office that first Monday morning after our return from Central America, my little house of cards started crumbling right in front of my eyes!

"You're fired, Weinstein! Now get your gear and get out of here!" I yelled at my private investigator. He had been stealing from me by hustling some of my cases off to other attorneys for a cut of the fee. And I hated to fire him because he knew too much about me. And as it turned out he later told the police everything he knew. And even made up a few little goodies just out of spite.

And Bob Bennett, the insurance adjuster who had set up the fraudulent insurance claims with me, was getting a little nervous. Some of the investigators from his national headquarters had come down and questioned him for days about some pretty suspicious looking claims he had paid off. And I figured he was going to break any second.

And my two gorillas, Big John and Blackie, were pushing me awfully hard for some money.

And an ex-cop who had been involved in one of the phony insurance claims was getting talkative because the police were coming around asking him questions about the "accident" he was in.

And I was getting followed a lot — day and night — by State and Federal Agents. That wouldn't have bothered me so much if they had just been cool about it. If they had just tried to not let me know. But they obviously didn't even care whether I saw them following me. And that meant they were onto something real heavy and were about to close in.

One night they followed me in my Mercedes half the night. I didn't dare go home because I had machine guns in the trunk and a plastic bag of cocaine in the front—and an expired inspection sticker on my windshield. And I just knew the moment I pulled in my driveway they'd bust me for the traffic offense and search the car. And that would be the end of that!

But I finally lost them.

Then I discovered the bugs on my phones. And I got a couple of tips from some insiders that I'd better go catch a slow boat to China.

But I didn't do it quite quickly enough.

And then that night came. That night to end all nights!

"Come on in, Bob" I answered the knock at my office door about six o'clock that evening. "I'm having a little tequila Marguerita. How about joining me?"

It was Bob Brandt, a lawyer friend of mine from the building, and his girlfriend. As sharp as Bob was, he had incredible weaknesses for liquor and drugs and girls. In that order. And he was always hanging around my offices to see if he could find any of the three of them. Which he frequently did.

"Yeah! How about a little old drink there, Counselor! It's been a long day, and I'm awful dry!"

But Bob was never dry. Because he started drinking down in Sally Russell's every morning about ten o'clock and didn't really slow down very much until around ten o'clock at night. And he would pop any pill he could get in his mouth or snort anything he could get through a soda straw.

But I liked him. And I trusted him.

I was bad about trusting folks.

"What do you think of this piece?" He asked with a strange look on his face as he plopped down in the chair across from my desk and handed me a .38 revolver which just seemed to materialize from nowhere.

"I don't know, man. What about it? There's nothing special about it." I said as I carefully avoided leaving my fingerprints on it anywhere and laid it back down on the desk in front of him.

"Aw nothin'. Just some guy gave it to me and I thought I'd ask." And all that sounded a little fishy to me. Then for the first time in the fifteen or twenty minutes that he had been in my office, I noticed his girlfriend was nowhere in sight.

And that really seemed fishy! And I started to say something. But just as I did, I heard the knock at the door.

My locked steel front door.

And Bob's girlfriend knew a whole lot better than to open my door at night just because someone was knocking. Nobody opened my door from the inside at night except me. And she knew that.

But she opened it.

That's why she was there.

And that's why Bob was there.

To let the police in!

And they came roaring in like a scene out of "The Untouchables!"

I never saw so many cops with drawn guns in my life.

And every gun was pointed right at my head!

"All right, up against the wall!" The little Latin American Federal Agent with the great big nickel-plated .357 magnum and the Cuban accent screamed at me as he lunged forward, poking the barrel into my face!

"—*you!*" He screamed again at the top of his voice! "Can't you understand English! I said, get up against that wall!"

And this time he shoved me up against the wall by the side of my desk with the gun at the back of my neck! And all the other agents poured into the office with their guns ready.

There must have been a dozen of them.

I didn't even think it was real for the first second or two because cops were always pulling that kind of trick in my office. Pointing guns and ordering me up against the wall and all that kind of funny stuff.

But now I knew they meant it! And it wasn't funny anymore!

As a couple of them held me against the wall at gunpoint and searched me thoroughly, the others started very systematically tearing the place apart. Looking for something. Looking for anything.

I remember Detective Ray Havens looked under the cushion in my chair twice for my pistol with the silencer. Because that's where I always kept it. And he knew it. And the reason he knew it was because my trusted friends and employees had both told him that was where I kept it.

But it just so happened it wasn't there.

And it just so happened the machine guns weren't down in the bottom of my breakfront where they usually were. And where the Federal Agents knew to look for them.

But as they handcuffed my hands behind my back and pushed me unceremoniously down into my chair, they really began going through the place.

And of course they didn't have a search warrant, so I reached up with my knee and flicked on the secret toggle switch under my desk which actuated the hidden tape re-corder. And I began very tactfully but very appropriately making all of the legal objections to their search and seizure. Laying the predicate for what I hoped to be a successful motion to suppress later on at a trial.

But they just kept on searching. And my objections only made them a little more angry. And they already hated me.

Bill Cagney, the Strike Force Prosecutor, came up and started jabbing his finger into my chest and screaming at me. "You big fat pig! *I'm gonna bury you!* I'm going to get you fifteen years on each of these counts! *I'm gonna bury you!* You're never comin' home, you fat pig!"

He was awfully brave when my hands were handcuffed behind my back and when there were about a dozen guys with guns standing around on his side!

Some of the agents from the Bureau of Narcotics and Dangerous Drugs vacuumed the entire suite of offices with a sterile vacuum cleaner, hoping to pick up some microscopic remains of marijuana or cocaine or whatever might have fallen into the nap of the carpet.

One of the agents even tore the Portuguese cork off of my wall, hoping to find something stashed in back of it.

188

And they confiscated my checkbooks and typewriter and dictating equipment and some of my files.

They even helped themselves to some of the cold beer in my refrigerator.

After an hour or so they finally discovered that my hidden tape recorder was very efficiently recording away every single word that was being spoken in the room. *And that really made them mad!*

And all this time, my "trusted" secretary was sitting downstairs with Neal Sonnet, the Chief Prosecutor in charge of the Criminal Prosecution Division of the United States Attorney's Office for the Southern District of Florida. Sipping martinis and having a good old time as the battle raged three floors above. Neal was one of my best friends. In fact he was about to run for State Attorney, and I had already promised to raise him a $50,000 campaign contribution from some of my "friends." But he was there tonight to see that I really got buried.

And the TV cameramen were right there along with him.

I can't really describe how I felt there that night. It's an incredible feeling! Unless you've been arrested and handcuffed and searched by a dozen Federal and State Agents with drawn guns—unless you've been a big man in the community who is suddenly crushed down by that kind of devastating force—you can never know what it feels like.

It's overwhelming —horrible and terrible and unforgettable!

But there it was — happening to me!

And yet it somehow seemed unreal. And for a few seconds every now and then I would think, *"Maybe this is not really happening! Maybe it's just a bad dream! Maybe it's a joke!"*

I guess they had been there for an hour or so before I thought of asking them to let me call my wife to get a bondsman and a lawyer for me.

"Me. Getting a bondsman!" I thought to myself. "And a lawyer! Isn't that incredible! This can't be happening. It just can't be happening!"

"Hello." I could hear the worry in Dorothy's voice over the phone. It was late and she knew something was wrong. Somehow, she always seemed to know.

"Honey . , . they've arrested me. They're here in the office right now, and they're about to take me to jail. You're going to have to get a bondsman for me. And a lawyer. Please call Chief Tracey and ask him to come down and make the bond. And call Bill Moran. And baby, I'm just so sorry. I'm so very sorry. Forgive me. Forgive me!"

"It's okay, Honey." She comforted me. "It's all right. Don't worry about it. I'll take care of it. I love you."

"Okay, baby. Thank you. I'm so very sorry." I hung up.

"All right. Let's go Neill!" One of the agents growled as he grabbed me by the arm and started ushering me out the door toward the elevator. They were just plain mad. And they didn't like me one little bit. It showed all over them. In fact, some of them really hated me. Like the little one in front with the big gun when they came in the room.

But I guess I don't really blame them. I wouldn't have liked me either.

In the middle of the back seat of the police car on the way to the Dade County Jail it still almost seemed unreal to me. My mind just wouldn't let me believe that it was really happening. And when we got there, they hustled me up the elevator to the Organized Crime Division of the Dade County Public Safety Department, and back in the back for fingerprinting and mugging.

But I refused to be fingerprinted or mugged. I particularly didn't want to be fingerprinted because I knew that was one of the only ways they could ever tie me in with that cocaine. By fingerprints. And I knew there wasn't a set of fingerprints in the world they could get into evidence unless they could get mine right now. And that made them madder. And madder.

But I don't really blame them. They were good cops. They were just doing their job. And I was a bad guy. So I'm not sore at them. And never was. Particularly Ray Havens and Jack Lloyd, the two Agents who really put me away.

After two or three hours up there in the Organized Crime Division they finally took me downstairs and around the outside of the building on the east side to bring me in for booking.

And there were the TV cameramen! Right on cue. And the two of them walked backwards down the sidewalk with their lights blinding my eyes as they filmed me for the fifty yard walk from the Detective Division to the Dade County Jail. They kept popping questions at me and trying to get me to say something. Or do something. Or to make a little action for their audience. But I was determined not to show any response of any kind. Until one of them finally got through to me.

"What do you think of the situation in the Far East?" He joked as the camera droned away in my face. And I had to chuckle. Because I had to admit that was a clever line.

But about that time we made it to the door of the jail, and they took me on inside and booked me. And that was *really humiliating!*

Because all of the police there were friends of mine and had been for many years. I knew every one of them by their first name. And I had always been the big shot to them. They'd looked up to me and treated me like I was some kind of hero. Some kind of Perry Mason.

But now here I was bleary-eyed and exhausted and handcuffed with my hands behind my back getting booked on three counts of sale of cocaine and one count of conspiracy.

When they finally put me in the hold cell back in the back with a couple of drunk blacks and several Puerto Ricans, I knew for the first time I was really a dead man.

That I was buried!

It really hit me there. Maybe it was the smell of the urine all over the floor or the stale tobacco stink or the cursing and filth and stench. Or maybe it was just because I was totally exhausted.

But it finally really hit me: *"You're a dead man!"*

And you'd be surprised how rapidly you degenerate in one of those holes.

The only place you can sit down in those hold cells is on a little six-inch board that protrudes out from the wall on both sides for six or eight feet. And when they first put me in there, both boards were filled with human bodies. Sitting there with their heads in their hands. Lost and sad and broken. And so I stood around. And I stood and stood. On one foot. And then on the other. I was just so tired!

"But I'll never sink to sitting down on the urine-soaked floor! I don't care how tired I get. I'm not going to become an animal like some of these scum in here!"

But I was just so tired.

And after a few hours I finally sank down to the floor.

And hours later, after all the others had bonded out, I was still in there alone when Detective Ray Havens and somebody else from the Organized Crime Division came by and looked into the cell.

"Hey Neill, did you know that Casey was a cop?" Havens laughed at me.

193

But I didn't answer.

And I think he kind of felt sorry for me.

But then they finally came and got me. I guess it must have been almost dawn. And it was old Chief Tracey who came. The bondsman whom I had used for all these years. Finally having to come and bond me out!

But Tracey was understanding and sympathetic, and he drove me all the way to my house in South Miami, some fifteen miles or so from the jail.

"Come on by the office in the next day or so, Gene, when you get a chance. When things have settled down a little." He asked me.

"Yeah, sure Chief. Thanks a million. I'll be there."

1 knew what he wanted. He wanted me to come by and pay the premium for the bond which he had just put up for me.

But it was a very low bond which had been set that night by a Federal Committing Magistrate who had been a friend of mine for many years. And who lived just around the corner from my house. He would have been awfully disappointed if he had known right then that I was going to jump bond and run in a few days!

Dorothy was waiting there at the door at home. I guess I never have known what went on inside her mind there that night. It must have been incredible. But it didn't show on her as I came in the door. She just put her arm around me and walked me back to the bedroom

194

and helped me into bed. She knew I was really beat. Beat mentally and emotionally and physically. Beaten all the way down.

"Baby, I'm just so very sorry." I kept repeating. *"I'm just so very sorry!"*

"It's all right, Gene, I love you. I love you." She whispered as I finally collapsed into sleep.

But from that moment on and for a long time, things just sort of went into a haze for me. Life was unreal and unearthly. I don't really know where I went or what I did or what I said. It was as though I were walking through some kind of strange dream. Some kind of strange nightmare.

I guess I called my partner Ray Glist and asked him to take over my practice for me. I don't really remember.

And I know I saw my lawyers, Bill Moran and Nick Tsamoutales the next day or so.

But I don't really remember that either.

Oh, I don't think it showed much. I could talk and function and think and act. And I'm sure I did so intelligently.

But I just don't remember all of it. And frankly I hope I never do.

I was a dead man. A man without a country. A man without a life. A man without hope.

Doomed.

"Why, of course!" It came to me like a bolt of lightning! "Why of course! Why didn't I think of that before!"

"I'll run! I can get out of here. I have enough money to go a long way. I'm smart, and I know all the ins and outs of criminal law. I know how cops chase robbers and where they chase them and when. They'll never catch me!"

My hope started picking up.

"Let's see... . I'll do it the way they would least expect me to. And I'll go in the fashion they would least expect me to go. And I'll go where they would least expect me to go."

"They would expect me to go first class wherever I was going. Maybe to Switzerland or Paris. Or maybe someplace where I would have more political sanctuary. Like Saudi Arabia."

"But I'll outsmart them. *I'll go as a bum! As a hippie!* Maybe in an old van. Across America, slowly over to the West Coast. And they'll never find me in a million years. I can go hide out for a few months in Gene Paris' cabin up in the mountains on Lake Blue Ridge in northern Georgia. And I'll grow a beard and long hair."

"Yeah, they'll never catch me in a million years!"

"Honey ... I'm going to run." I almost apologized to Dorothy one night. "I won't tell you where I'm going because that would put you on the spot. But I'm going to leave tonight, and I'll get someplace very safe and secure. And then I'll get word back to you somehow, and you can bring the kids and come meet me. *But, baby, you're going to have to be awfully careful!* Because they're going to watch you every second for the rest of your life until they catch me! They're really going to go right up the wall when they find out I'm gone. And the judge is probably going to get a lot of heat for having set such a low bond. But that's his problem; I've got my own."

"Oh honey, I'm so scared!" Dorothy said. "Don't run! Can't we do something else instead? Isn't there some other way out?" She started to cry.

"It's the only way, love. It's the only way."

And so I slipped out of the house undetected by the police who kept a constant vigil across the street. And I made it down to a pay phone on South Dixie Highway where I knew the line wasn't bugged.

And I called Gene Paris. Good old Gene! He was my first wife's stepbrother. And he and I had been best friends for twenty years. I would have trusted him with my life. He was intelligent and clever, and I really believed he would have done anything in the world to help me get away. He would have died for me. The best friend I ever had.

And he was an atheist. Just like me. His mother was a sweet little Baptist lady, and we used to tease her, good naturedly, about God and the Bible. And of her going to church.

And, like me, Gene had had wealth, influence, power and education. He had been a big man in Atlanta. He and his family had owned East Point Ford Company, one of the most profitable Ford companies in

197

the city at one time. And he had had everything you can buy with money.

But then one day — since I had seen him face to face the last time — he had gotten completely wiped out! In a period of just a few weeks he lost his Ford agency and his wife and child, and his house and car and bank account. Everything.

And just once in a while — not always — that will make a man seek more eternal and lasting values for his life.

And it had him.

But I didn't know about that as I dialed his number that night.

"Hello there 'Ace'!" I tried to sound jovial. "This is your wayward lawyer friend down here in Miami. Have you read the papers in Atlanta recently?"

"Oh man! What are we gonna do!" He commiserated.

"You're gonna pick me up there in the airport in Atlanta when I get off of Delta flight 647 at 9:50 tonight. That's what we're gonna do. How about it? And I'll explain the rest to you when I get there."

"I'll be there. Come on. Is there anything else I can do?"

"Yeah! You can go out and buy a step van for me. One that's kind of beat-up looking on the outside but real good mechanically. One that would make a good camper to cross America in. See what you can find, and I'll meet you there at the airport."

"Okay, Gene. I'll see you there. Be careful. Goodbye."

"Goodbye."

And I grabbed a taxi to the Miami International Airport. But I went through the terminal with dark glasses on, moving just as quickly as I could, because the place is always crawling with cops. And all of them knew me by my first name.

"Whew! Nobody saw me." I breathed a sigh of relief as I settled into my seat on the airplane. *I was on my way to freedom!*

And I planned my escape all the way to Atlanta. There was just no way I was going to get caught.

"Hello there, Ace!" I happily greeted Gene Paris. "Happily" because a tremendous burden had been lifted off me. I was on my way to freedom!

But then Gene Paris did a strange thing. He threw his arms around me as he ran up to me there in the airport. And he said, "God bless you, Gene! I love you. And I'm glad to see you!" And he hugged me and kissed me on the cheek.

This wasn't the same Gene Paris I had known for twenty years.

This was a new Gene Paris. Filled with a new kind of love. A new joy and a new kind of peace. And talking about a God! And I could tell he was happier now than I had ever seen him — though he had almost none of the worldly goods he had once had.

"Oh boy — I wonder what's happened to Gene!" I remember thinking to myself as we got into his car and started driving. And as we drove towards his little apartment in East Point where he and his new wife Cindy were living, I told him a part of my plan. I told him about going as a hippy and how I was going to head out West because they wouldn't be looking for me that way.

"Yeah! Okay — fine, Gene." He agreed with me. "That sounds great. And I'll go down first thing in the morning and pick up a van. And you can be on your way up to our cabin for a couple of months. And you know how deserted that place is! You could spend the rest of your life up there and never see anybody!"

But as we parked outside of his little apartment, I had no idea that the *greatest moment of truth in my whole life* was about to come upon me. My life was about to change. Dramatically and incredibly.

Because of this one man's faith in an Almighty God!

After I greeted Cindy, Gene and I went back into the bedroom so he could change clothes. He had on a suit, and he was going to put on some dungarees. And as we stood there in the bedroom chatting, he began emptying his pockets onto the bureau and changing clothes.

But when I looked down at his change on the bureau, *I saw something I would never have expected to see in Gene Paris' pocket!*

A tiny cross!

A cheap little aluminum cross about an inch and a quarter high. With four little words stamped on the front:

200

"Jesus Christ is Lord"

And I thought, "What in the world is he doing with *that* in his pocket!"

"Gene, what's this thing for?" I frowned at him.

"Gene, I've changed," was his simple reply. "I'm a Christian now. And I'd like to pray for you." He said with tears welling up in his eyes. Tears of love and compassion and understanding. And he put his arm around me and took me into the next room and he prayed.

A simple little prayer.

"Oh dear Father, come help my friend!" He wept as he prayed. "Come help my friend. Come help my friend."

Oh I'd heard people pray before. Like in the mammoth, multi-million dollar First Methodist Church of Coral Gables where I grew up. Where they told me that the Bible didn't really mean what it said. And where nobody ever really talked about Jesus.

"Our Father who art in heaven.. .," they would drone on in a fast monotone. Just trying to get it over as quickly as they could. "Hallowed be thy name...." But nobody in the whole huge cathedral was really praying that the name of God should be hallowed above every name.

"Thy kingdom come. . . , they would continue in fast unison. But the only thing they were really wishing would come was twelve o'clock.

So they could get out of there and get on over to the country club. Or out to the yacht club. Or home to roast beef.

And I remember the pastor used to pray too. But they were always written prayers. Prayers designed to have the greatest possible psychological effect on the congregation. Prayers mostly about money and buildings and expansion programs.

"Heaping up empty phrases. ..."

But I'd never really heard anybody pray like there was truly a God somewhere listening. A God they knew would answer them. And I'd never seen anyone weep as he prayed.

And it changed my life.

I still didn't believe there was a God. I thought poor Gene Paris was just mistaken. But all of a sudden a feeling came over me that if I would just go back to Miami and plead guilty to all these crimes — everything would be all right. Everything would be all right!

It was a crazy feeling. Absolutely insane. It had no logic to it. It had no reason to it. It went totally and completely contrary to every intelligent thought that I had in my mind.

Because I was free now. I knew I was on my way. I knew there was no way I could get caught.

And yet the urge overwhelmed me: "Go on back home. Admit to everything. Plead guilty. And everything will be all right."

202

I didn't know at that time that every human being has both a mind and a spirit. And I didn't know the two are frequently pulling in opposite directions.

"Gene, I know it sounds crazy." I said to Gene Paris a little later. "But I'm going to go on back to Miami. I'm going to go on back and plead guilty. I'm going to confess to the things I've done. And don't ask me why. But I have a crazy feeling all of a sudden that if I'll go back and plead guilty — everything is going to be all right. I know it's crazy — but I just have a feeling."

"Praise the Lord!" He exclaimed. "I'm going back with you!" And he jumped up out of his chair and got ready to walk with me back out the front door.

He hadn't tried to talk me out of running. He was going to help me get away. And he would have done whatever he had to do to help me.

But I guess whoever it was that was putting that feeling in me — that I should go back — was putting the same feeling in him.

That great Whoever frequently does that kind of thing.

And so we went back to the airport. I even had to buy his plane ticket because he didn't have enough money. But he had riches I didn't even know about yet.

I still didn't believe there was a God. I was still an atheist. I absolutely did not believe there was a God anyplace. I was only going back because the feeling was just overwhelming!

And I called the Committing Magistrate from Atlanta — the one who had set the bond on me — and I told him that I was guilty. That I had run. And that I was sorry. And that I was coming back to confess and to plead guilty.

So I went back. And I called Bill Cagney, the Special Washington Strike Force Prosecutor.

"Bill, this is Gene Neill. I'm guilty of those things that I got arrested for. And I want to come in and make a statement. I want to plead guilty."

"Yeah, sure. Well, er, uh. Well, just come on into the office tomorrow morning." He stammered. He was absolutely flabbergasted! He couldn't believe I was pleading guilty. And I couldn't believe it either.

But I went in all right.

Right into the office of the Federal Strike Force in Miami. And boy, were they waiting for me! There must have been about nine agents. One or two from each of the Federal agencies in whose jurisdictions I had committed crimes. And they had a Court Reporter. They sat me down and swore me in and started firing questions at me. Fast. Tough questions. Devastating questions!

And I answered every one of them, for I think three days. It seemed like a lifetime.

And it almost cost me the rest of my life!

After I was all through giving my statements there to the Strike Force, I called my lawyers and told them what I had done. *And they went right up the wall!*

Bill Moran and Nick Tsamoutales were probably the two most effective criminal lawyers in Miami in those days. And they were all ready to fight.

"Man, we can beat these cases!" Bill Moran almost cried.

"Yeah, and they'll be filing more, now that I've told them about the rest of the things I've been doing." I shrugged sheepishly to Bill.

And did they ever!

My name had been on the front page of the Miami Herald for almost a week after I got arrested. And they had mentioned me on TV every day. But now there were new headlines. About machine guns and insurance frauds and pistols with silencers. And all kinds of other things.

And now there was nothing to do but sit around and wait. Wait for them to bring me up for sentencing. And I waited. And waited. And waited. I guess it must have been about three months.

I couldn't sleep. I couldn't work, I couldn't go anywhere. I couldn't do anything.

Just sit and think.

But then the day finally came!

And they called me up as a defendant before Judge C. Clyde Atkins, one of the Federal District Judges there in Miami for the Southern District of Florida. A Roman Catholic fellow. And he did what he had to do.

As I stood there before him, pleading guilty to all of the many counts, my wife stood there with me with her arm around me. And after I had pleaded guilty, she looked up at me with big tears in her eyes. And she said, "Honey, I've never been as proud of you in my life."

But she knew I was going away.

Judge Atkins only sentenced me under the indictment for the sale of the cocaine. He held the others aside for the time being.

But the cocaine indictment contained three counts of illegal transfer and one count of conspiracy. And the transfers carry a maximum of fifteen years apiece and the conspiracy five. And three times fifteen is forty-five, plus five equals fifty.

And that's what he gave me. Under Section 4208 (b).

Fifty years.

Fifty years!!

And he sent me out to the Federal Penitentiary in Springfield, Missouri. Probably one of the most maximum security Federal institutions in America. And probably one of the worst. Because it's where they send the psychos. And where they send the men they're just going to bury. The men who are going to be there forever. Old men. Broken men. Sick men.

It's a terrible place.

When the Marshalls pulled up out in front of the Penitentiary there with me in the back seat, I was wearing Martin chains. A chain around my waist and my hands shackled to that chain. They took me down into a tunnel in the ground. An underground passageway where they bring all the incoming prisoners. And when we got down inside the first little room they sat me down on a bench there. And there was another man already sitting there who had arrived a few moments before I did.

I was dressed in a business suit and a necktie and a clean shirt. Well groomed. But this other poor devil was wretched looking and dirty. And so very lonely.

And one of the guards started questioning him and filling in the blank spaces on the admission sheet. I was only about half listening because I was thinking mostly about me. But then all of a sudden I heard a question and an answer that hit me like a thunderclap.

"Have you ever been here to Springfield before?"

"Oh man, I don't know. I've been in so many of these joints ... I don't know. Probably."

He didn't even know!

He didn't even remember whether he had been to this prison before!

My God, My God! How low can a man sink! I thought. Here it was - the most traumatic and most horrible experience of my entire lifetime - walking in that front door and letting it slam behind me! A moment I could never forget in a million years. And yet - here was a man who had been around these places so much he couldn't even remember whether he had ever been there before!

"That's what I'll be like fifty years from now" I thought. "It won't matter. I won't even care."

And then my turn came.

They took my clothes off of me and searched me while I was naked. A horribly humiliating and degrading experience.

And then they put me in a shower and watched me while I bathed. When I got through bathing, they put a uniform on me—just a pair of pants and a shirt. No shoes or socks or underwear or belt.

And the pants were size 54" in the waistline. I had to keep holding them up with my hand to keep them from falling down. The guards all laughed at me. They thought that was so amusing.

But I was starting to cry.

Then all of a sudden, there I was - back in my little cell.

I guess I had been sort of daydreaming for many hours. My whole life had gone by me. And I had seen it in all of its sad reality. All its failure.

And I had seen myself. I guess for the first time in my life I had really seen myself. A broken old man. A tragic, decadent, lonely old failure.

All alone. For fifty years.

You'd be surprised how insignificant and unimportant my Mercedes seemed to me now. Or the airplane. Or money. Or law degree.

In the final moment of truth — only one thing in life has any intrinsic value at all. And that is — is there really, really a God someplace? A real God? Not just a God concept, like many churches speak of so loosely. But a real living God?

Does He know I'm down here in this terrible little hole? Does He know that I'm sorry?

Does He care?

Will He come help me?

I was forty years old when I entered that cell. I had been all over the world. Grew up in a church. I'd been to places many people have never even heard of. And I'd done things few have ever done. I was well educated and well-rounded and articulate and sensitive.

But in all the world, no man had ever looked me in the face and said, " Gene, there's a real living Lord Jesus Christ - Who loves you and Who died for you."

In all the world, no man had ever said to me, "Gene, there's a real God. And He's not just a concept or a word that you banter around. But He's real and alive and He loves you, and He cares for you and wants you to be His."

I had never heard those words. Anywhere!

And I kept thinking about Gene Paris in Atlanta. And how he had prayed:

"Oh, heavenly Father! Please, come help my friend!"

I thought about how he had cried when he prayed. And though I thought he was wrong — I knew from the bottom of my heart that *he believed there was a real God someplace*! A real God who heard his voice and who was going to answer his prayer. A God who loved him. And who loved me. I knew he believed that.

"Oh, my God, my God!" I said to myself. *"What if I'm wrong!* What if there really is a God someplace. What if somewhere way out beyond the stars there's a big room up there in the sky somewhere — a great big room with a throne in it, and a God sitting on the throne who can hear prayers. Who can even hear me all the way down here! What if I'm wrong! What if He really *is* there!"

And so, lonely and terrified and desperate, and hot and sweaty and dirty, I threw myself down on the floor of that little cell. And I called out to that God that I didn't believe in. I called out to that God, just hoping that maybe — *just maybe* — He might be in that room somewhere out beyond the stars.

"Oh, my God, my God!" I cried. "What have I done!"

"God, I just don't think you're out there. I'm sorry, but I just don't think you're there. But God, if you really are there, if you really are there somewhere -- someplace out there, and if you can hear me - dear God, I'm sorry. Dear God, I'm so sorry! Just as sorry as I can be. Oh, God, please forgive me! Please forgive me!"

"God, if you're really out there someplace, if you're really there, and if somehow you can hear my voice, and if you'll just give me one last chance - I promise I'll never ask you for anything else as long as I live. Nothing! And God, I promise you that if you'll just give me one more chance, I'll never do anything bad again. Never God. Never. I promise!"

"But if you're really out there . . . if you could just somehow let me start my life over somehow - brand new - God, I'll stay here in this little cell. And I'll do this whole fifty years! Or I'll go home with my kids if you want me to. I'll do whatever you want me to do."

"But if you're really out there - please come help me! Please, God, come help me! Oh God, come help me! Oh God, come help me!"

"Oh God!"

13   "HE LIVES! HE LIVES!"

"Gene, I love you." I heard the words in a beautiful deep melodious voice that was just filled with love.

"And I have waited a long time for you." He continued gently. "But if you will really give me your life - I will give you my life."

Oh what a voice it was! Just so filled with love and understanding and kindness and tenderness. He wasn't angry at me. He felt sorry for me. And He loved me and wanted to help me. The same God that made little roses and big mountains and oceans and puppy dogs — loved me! *And He was alive and real, and He could hear my prayers!*

He really cared. And He came down into that little solitary cell with me and just lifted me up off the floor. He held me up to Himself and comforted me.

And He gave me a chance to start my life all over. Brand new. Just like I had been born all over again.

I'm an educated, traveled and intelligent man. But I don't have any idea what God did in my life there on that little cell floor.

All I know is that one moment I was terrified and running over with sorrow. Heaped up with sin and torn by loneliness.

But when I called His name — He answered me. And He forgave me. I found what I had looked all over the world for. What I had searched for in Europe and the Far East. And in wealth and power and influence.

I found peace. Love and joy and peace.

A peace that really does pass all human understanding.

And I don't know how it works. All I know is that it does.

There was a man one time who had been born blind. And a man named Jesus came along and touched him and healed his eyes. He could see! But the religious leaders became angry, and they called the man who had been blind to the temple and demanded, "Who is this Jesus? What has He done? And how did He do it?"

But the man just answered, "I don't know."

"I don't know. All I know is once I was blind, but now I can see!"

Beloved — all I know is that once I lay there in dust — *life's glory dead. But from the ground there blossomed red, life that shall endless be.*

And I made a solemn vow to God there that day on that little cell floor.

"Father," I said, "I don't know what you want of me here in this prison. And I don't know what you want of my life. But I make you a promise right now that *for the rest of my life* — every second, every minute, every hour, every day — I'm going to try to be just as much like your son Jesus as I possibly can. I know I can't be just like Him. But I promise you with all my heart, *I'm going to try! I promise you, Father."*

And I became just totally overwhelmed with the feeling of His presence right there in my cell. I could feel Jesus taking over my very life. I could feel the Holy Spirit coming into my life and giving me His strength and power and comfort. And His gifts! And enriching my life with the fruit of His Spirit!

And I knew He lived!

And because I knew He lived, I could face tomorrow. All fear was gone. I could do that fifty year sentence in that solitary cell, for I had conquered the world in that infinite instant of time when God made me His! I had conquered the world — and life and death. And I held eternity in the palm of my hand.

When I finally got up off of my knees, probably several hours later, my tiny cell looked somehow different. It was still the same size. It was still filthy. And I still had fifty years to go. But there was peace there now. And comfort and security. And I was happy.

215

I was *really* happy for the very first time in my whole life! A new kind of happiness that was real and solid. And which I knew was going to last forever. I just somehow knew.

So in my own stumbling way, I began thanking God and praising Him. I began seeking Him and His righteousness. I began trying to be like Jesus.

Over and over I kept singing, "Lord, I want to be like Jesus. In'a my heart. In'a my heart. Lord, I want to be a Christian. In'a my heart. In'a my heart."

And although we weren't allowed to have anything there in that little cell, God miraculously provided me with a King James Bible. I had the advantage of not knowing anything at all about it. The advantage of not having had any man teach me what it did — or didn't — mean. So I just started reading it. And believing it. *Every single word of it!*

And I believe every word of it today.

I believe that it is the inspired, absolute, infallible, verbatim, total Word of an Almighty God who loves me. And who knows my name. And who gave me one last chance there on that little solitary cell floor.

And the whole reason He gave us His Holy Bible was so that people like me — in prison cells — or people who are in prison cells in their hearts — can just take His Book and start reading it. And if they will only believe it — they can live a life filled with all the victory and triumph and the joy and power of our Lord Jesus Christ! As He lived

216

when He was here on earth. They too can conquer the world. And life and death. And sickness and sorrow and pain. They can have everlasting joy!

And never want for anything!

Just by reading it. And believing it.

I remember God somehow directed my eyes that first day to what is probably the most cosmic and vital and dynamic promise that has ever been made in all the infinite universes. And that promise says that,

.. . neither death, nor life, nor angels, nor powers, nor things present, nor things to come, nor height, nor depth, nor any other creature, shall be able to separate us from the love of God, which is in Christ Jesus our Lord (Romans 8:38, 39).

And I knew it meant that prison cells and fifty year sentences and all the horrors that go with them could not separate me from the love of that God who had come down and touched my heart there on that floor! I knew that all the love that He had — all the love that He had — was in that little cell with me.

Then my eyes flicked up the page a little way to another promise. A promise that is so infinite in its scope it transcends all human comprehension. That,

... all things work together for good to them that love God. . . (Romans 8:28).

And so I knew that somehow — someway — God was going to make that prison cell and that fifty years and that horrible place work together for good. Somehow. I just knew He would!

And then I began reading the Bible right from the front cover. Because I figured that's where you ought to start reading any book. And I read it all the way through. I guess in less than a week. Then I read it through again. And again. And again. And it became a part of me.

When the guards would bring my food three times a day and set it on the floor just outside my cell, I had to get down on my knees and reach out and slide it in to eat it. But I always tried to say something nice to them each time. I tried to let them see Jesus in my life. I tried to say things which I thought maybe Jesus would say if He were there on His knees in front of them.

And after they would leave, I would sit there and eat the food with thanksgiving. Usually with my fingers, because we weren't allowed to have silverware. Sometimes there was a paper spoon. But a lot of times there was nothing.

But I began always and for everything giving thanks in the name of our Lord Jesus Christ to God my Father. I just rejoiced always. *Always!* And I had no anxiety about anything. But in everything, by prayer and supplication and with great thanksgiving, I would let my requests be made known to my heavenly Father. And I prayed *constantly. And gave thanks in all circumstances.* For I knew that was the will of God in Christ Jesus for me. And I knew that if I would do that, the peace of God which passes all under-standing would indeed keep my heart and my mind in Christ Jesus.

And it did!

After a couple of weeks they took me in for a hearing before a board of about six men and one woman. And I knew that the idea was for them to try to decide then and there how much time I should have to spend in the penitentiary.

As I entered the room, they had already examined my file and were all looking up at me.

Angrily.

"Neill, do you think fifty years is a reasonable sentence for you?" The leader of the panel asked coldly.

"Well, sir," I tried to answer calmly, "I know the things I did were horrible things. Terrible things. But I feel God has forgiven me for them now, and I just can't say that fifty years is a reasonable period of time. Because it's just so long. *It's just so awfully long!*"

And I guess I stammered as I tried to get the words out.

The woman on the panel was a former Marine. And she grabbed the file from the chairman, glanced at it a second, and then growled at me sarcastically, "Well do you think thirty-five years would be reasonable, Neill?"

"Ma'am, I don't know," I tried to show her love as I answered, "it just seems like such an awfully long time. I'm not saying I don't deserve it. I'm just saying that it seems like such a long time."

"Well, I can see there's no need in even talking to you!" She blew up as she threw the file into a cardboard box by the table. "Get out!"

There went my chance of ever going home. But I had tried to be honest. I had tried to say what I thought Jesus would say.

But I went back to my little cell and started praising God all over again and thanking Him and rejoicing. And reading the Bible some more.

About a week later, they transferred me to another solitary cell. Exactly the same size. Same layout. But it had a cot with springs. And it was a little bit cleaner. And it had a window I could see out of into a little courtyard down below. I couldn't see out into the free world. But there was a little tree down there. A little dead tree. And from that little cell I wrote a poem to God. Because I loved Him so. And it goes like this:

I'M FREE

My prison home is cold and gray and made of rock and steel;

it's filled with tears both night and day with little love to feel.

The sick and sad and broken men who suffer here with me

cannot recall the moment when they last were glad and free.

They can't recall the trees and flowers

nor sun nor stars nor moon;

barbed wire and high foreboding towers

shut all out but the doom.

Yet I am happy and I'm free

though tombed within this hell,

for mighty acts of God I see through cold bars of my cell.

For sparrows play outside my wall

and flit from fence to tree.

I know He grieves their every fall,

and He is here with me!

And He was!

And I knew that indeed everything was going to work out all right.
And though Dorothy couldn't visit me, I wrote her every day and told
her about His love and about the peace that I had there.

After a few weeks, they started letting me come out of my cell to take my meals in the chow hall. *What a joy it was to have all that new "freedom."* And silverware. I remember my first meal there. I had stood in the chow line for a long time — perhaps a half an hour — waiting to get up to where the food was. And suddenly a burly looking old man butted in line in front of me just as I got to the food.

But I didn't say anything to him. I loved him and felt sorry for him. But out of curiosity I turned to the man in back of me.

"Who's this guy?" I asked nodding back over my shoulder to the old man.

"Oh, that's just Old John. He used to be a hit man for 'Murder, Incorporated!' But when you've been here thirty-five years — you can go to the head of the chow line too!" He whispered fatalistically.

There in the chow hall — for the first time — I got an opportunity to get a good look at "convicts." There were probably three or four hundred of them in there at all times during the meal hours.

And what a terrible sight!

Most of the men were sick and gray and ugly and dirty.

And there were a lot of *"girls"* — as they called themselves. Men who wore homemade lipstick and brassieres and cut their pant legs off real short. And who wore their hair long and carried homemade purses slung over their shoulders.

And the venereal disease rate was *incredibly* high.

222

But the guards just laughed at it and did nothing to discourage it.

A lot of the men were always getting in fights and screaming and cursing each other. Loathsome words! Incredibly loathsome words.

It's a real cesspool of humanity.

Then one night a fellow cut his wrists, and I guess died. I don't know. But they moved me upstairs to the second floor into his cell the next day. And it was *splattered all over with blood*. They had gotten some of it up off the floor. But it was all over the walls and the bed and sink and toilet. And they told me to clean it up.

And then Christmas came.

My first Christmas in prison. And boy was it tough! At Christmas time your thoughts really go back home to your wife and kids. And to your mother and the rest of your family. They go all the way back to your childhood days when your mother used to rock you in her lap in front of the Christmas tree and sing songs to you.

And in prison, Christmas day is the *worst day of all*. It's the day that more men get in fights and more men get killed than any other day.

There was snow on the ground outside Christmas Eve. The lights just shimmered and sparkled off the snow like myriads of diamonds! And there was a little rabbit outside my cell window who lived in a drainage pipe that opened up right in the middle of the little courtyard. And there he was out there in the moonlight. In the snow. Nibbling away at some little ends of grass.

And I sang hymns that night to my heavenly Father. Hymns that I had learned as a little boy and hardly remembered the words to. Like *Away in a Manger. It Came Upon a Midnight Clear.* And *Silent Night.* I sat there in my little cell and sang and sang in whispers to the God who loved me. And who was there with me.

Oh, I wasn't really sad. I missed my wife and children and my mother. But I wasn't really sad because God was there with me in a powerful and intimate and warm and loving way. And I knew He was never going to leave me, and I knew He'd want me to be happy on His Son's birthday.

But some of the men tried to kill themselves that Christmas Eve.

One man swallowed a tablespoon to try to kill himself. When that didn't work, he folded up a coat hanger and swallowed it. And when that didn't kill him, he took the long zigzag spring out of his bed and folded it up and swallowed it.

But I was happy. And I never tried to get out of prison. I never even asked God to take one second off my sentence. Because I had promised Him that I would stay right there and do all that time if He wanted me to. And I never asked men to let me out. Or to try to get me out.

Then one day a guard yelled, "Neill, get your things ready. The Marshalls are comin' for ya! They'll be here in twenty minutes. Report on down to 'Receiving and Discharge' on the double!"

"Where are they taking me?" I asked dumbly. Because you never know. They're always moving prisoners about and sending them

224

from one penitentiary to another. Always moving them. Even from one cell to another.

"Back to Miami for a *Writ of Habeas Corpus ad Testificandum*." The guard yelled back over his shoulder as he walked away.

"Ad Testificandum!" I thought. "That means they're taking me back to testify against somebody! Who do they want me to testify against! I don't want to testify against anybody!"

My mind raced back and forth over all the possibilities as I grabbed my few belongings together and headed for R&D.

So they packed up my Bible and my new toothbrush, safety razor and shaving brush — which I was allowed to have now that I was out "in population." And they gave me my old "street clothes" to put back on. The clothes that I had worn in there fifty-five days earlier.

But I really looked like a clown! I had lost fifty-five pounds in the first fifty-five days, and the suit hung over me like a potato sack.

But then they came for me. And any convict can tell you when the Marshalls arrive. You're always sitting in the hold cell waiting. But you can hear them. Because you can hear their chains rattling. They always have their chains. Their Martin chains and handcuffs and leg irons.

And they came in and put the chains on me and led me outside to their car. Out in the crisp and frosty and beautiful sunshiny morning.

They put me in the back seat of their car with another prisoner and drove us for hours and hours. Until we finally pulled up in the dirty and dreary looking parking lot of the Wyandotte County Jail in Kansas City, Kansas. *Probably one of the worst jails in America.*

The guards booked us in and unshackled us and started taking the two of us back into our dungeon-like little cell.

Then we saw her.

A pretty looking girl about sixteen or seventeen. She was scared and frightened and shaking like a little doe deer. Sitting there in her cell all alone.

"Ah ha!" The filthy minded guard roared as he unlocked the barred door. "I'm going to put these two animals in here with you, baby, and just let them do whatever they want! Ha!"

"Oh, no! Please!" Terror swept her little face as her hand shot up over her mouth in fear.

But then he slammed the barred door back shut again and locked it.

He was only kidding.

Or at least *this time* he was. But sometimes they aren't kidding when they do things like that.

And he led us on down to the last cell in the building. *And it was just filthy beyond belief.* A six-foot three- inch steel ceiling, four steel slab bunks, steel walls, steel floor, totally covered with human excrement and urine. *And cockroaches everywhere!* There was a toilet out in the middle of the floor and there must have been two hundred cockroaches crawling all over it. And on the floor all around it. And there wasn't any toilet paper. *It was suffocating and hot and it stunk!* Loathsome and detestable.

But I took my clothes off and lay down in the filth and squalor and cockroaches. And I slept like a little baby. Because Jesus was with me.

"Okay, Neill - let's go!" The guard yelled at me early the next morning. *"Get out here!"*

I pulled on my clothes hurriedly and followed him out of the cell. And I smiled and waved at the young girl as I passed her cell, trying to bring a little joy into her life. She was still sitting right where she had been when I passed her the evening before.

Then the Marshalls drove me out to the airport. And I must have really looked a sight to the free world people there in the lobby of the airport as they brought me in, in chains. Filthy, unshaven, and in clothes several sizes too big for me! Men frowned angrily at me. Women turned their heads. Children whispered to their parents.

But I wanted to tell them about Jesus and about His love. But I couldn't.

On the plane, the Marshalls sat on each side of me, back in the back where the stewardesses ride. And we were off to Miami.

After landing at the Miami International Airport, they loaded me into another Marshall's car and drove me back to the Dade County Jail, where I was booked and fingerprinted and mugged for the umpteenth time. Again by the officers who used to know me when I was a big man around town.

But now I was just another dirty convict.

After many hours in the smelly hold cell there, they finally transported me by prison truck out to the Dade County Stockade on the outskirts of town. My home for the next three months.

And I followed a guard through a high and barbed-wire topped chain link fence into the maximum security Federal holding cell there in the Stockade. One little cell with thirty-two big and loud and smelly convicts.

But as miserable as the conditions were, and as rotten as the food was, and as humiliating and degrading as that kind of imprisonment is — *I was happy. Because I knew my Jesus was with me and that He was going to take care of me. Forever!*

Then I saw Dorothy for the first time! Through the fence about a hundred yards away! And I waved at her and she waved at me. And it was like Christmas and New Year's and gas-filled balloons and merry-go-rounds and calliopes and cotton candy all in one second! Because I had a new kind of love. Not only for all of humanity — but even a new kind for her, too!

We got to visit for two hours each weekend — across a railing and a chain link fence — a safe seven feet apart. But we were so much in love!

Dorothy had not yet met the risen Lord Jesus. But she saw the incredible transformation that had taken place in my life. And she immediately began seeking His Kingdom and His righteousness.

They never did call me into court to testify against anyone.

But then another miracle began! God began to get me out!

"Neill, report to R & D in the morning at five!" The guard yelled through the bars of my cell late one night.

"Why! Where am I going?" I urged back through the darkness toward the sound of the voice.

"I dunno. They didn't tell me. Just be there!"

But it wasn't to testify. It was Judge Atkins who was ordering me back. And he was going to re-sentence me!

"Four years!" He said. Hallelujah! Only four years!

Four years under United States Code Section 4208(a) (1)! And that would make me "eligible" for parole after only one more year!

Praise the Lord! *"So if the Son makes you free, you will be free indeed!"*

God had already set me free in the most important sense, free from the world and from care and sorrow and sadness. *But now He was getting ready to swing open those gates!*

I was also sentenced under the other two indictments for the machine guns and for the insurance frauds —*four* years on each case.

"Where do I go from here?" I asked the Chief Deputy Marshall through the bars of the holding cage, where they were holding me in back of the courtrooms after the sentencing.

"Who knows! Maybe back to Springfield, Atlanta, Texarcana. Who knows!" He answered without even looking up from his desk.

"What about Eglin? Can I get sent to Eglin? Is there any chance they would send me there?" I hoped out loud.

"No chance! Not till you're down to two years. You've got too much time yet. Maybe after a couple of years. Maybe." He still didn't even look up.

I had heard Eglin was as good a place to do time as any around. And you could visit with your wife and family on Saturdays and Sundays. And that's what I wanted. And that's what I prayed that night.

"Dear Father, you've been so awfully good to me. And I love you so much! And I thank you for what you've done.

"And I'm not going to ask you for anything just for me. But for my wife and kids' sake, Father, please let me go to Eglin. Please let me go to Eglin. So I can be with them. God, please let me go to Eglin!" I really prayed.

But weeks went by. With no word about anything.

Then one night, dear little eighty-year-old Dr. Chuckmakis checked into the Stockade on a court call. He was a prisoner — back from *Eglin!*

"I heard them talking about you up there!" He smiled at me enthusiastically. "In the parole records office. And they said they'd like for you to come up there because you're a lawyer, and you can type, and they need some clerks up there. But they said you might not be able to *because you have too much time.* You're not down to two years. But I think maybe you'll get to go. Just watch and see!" The old Greek physician-convict tried to reassure me.

And then the news came! About midnight one night,

"Clang! Clang! Clang!" The guard's stick rang out against the bars of my cell window! "Neill, where are ya! Wake up in there Neill! Neill!"

He didn't know which bunk I was in. And he wasn't about to come in that dark cell with thirty-two convicts in the middle of the night. But what he didn't know was that my bunk was right beside the window he was banging on. And I came about three feet up off of it when he yelled my name!

"Yes! Yes! Here I am!" I spurted out groggily.

231

"You're goin' to Eglin in the morning,' Neill! Be down at R & D at five!"

"Yes, sir!"

I thought I was going to soar right on up through the ceiling! *"Thank you Lord God! Thank you Father. Thank you Father. Thank you Father!"* I kept repeating over and over until I dropped off to sleep again.

And there they were with their chains again the next morning. The Marshalls with their Martin chains. And they chained up three of us and put us in the back seat of a little Chevy two-door and headed north.

They finally let us out of the car for the first time late that evening, in a small town jail in north Florida. They put the three of us in a cell with a couple of other convicts in transit. And the place was clean enough, for a change. But we didn't get any sleep all night.

There were three women in the cell right next to us, and although we couldn't see them, we could hear them clearly enough.

Boy, could we hear them!

"No! No! Please don't. Oh that hurts!" One of them kept pleading over and over as the other two assaulted her.

"Oh my God, my God, let me out of here!" Another one screamed from another cell all night! "Oh guards - come let me out of here! I'm a poor old crippled woman! Been crippled all my life. Oh guards, come let me out of here! Oh, help, help, God come get me out of here! Oh, help me!" All night, over and over.

And every once in a while the guard would bellow out in a deep and ethereal voice over the loud public address system, *"MAAAAGGGIEE! Oh Maggie! This is God, Maggie! This is God, Maggie! Shut up in there, Maggie. This is God. Shut up!"*

I guess he seriously thought he was going to fool her.

"Oh, let me out of here. I'm a poor old crippled woman!" He didn't fool her.

But then the next afternoon — there was Eglin!

The Eglin Federal Prison Camp. On the Eglin Air Force Base outside of Fort Walton Beach, Florida. Forty miles east of Pensacola. Way off on the edge of the Air Force Base out in the swamps. Filled with cockroaches and mosquitoes and flies and frogs and rain and summer heat.

But it looked like paradise to me. After what I'd been through it looked like Holy Ground. And it turned out to be just that. At least for me.

A kind old convict named John checked me in. For a lost man he was one of the nicest men I'd ever met in my life. Always trying to help people. Always smiling. Always had a glad word.

233

I would never have guessed, as he checked me in that day, that I would write his epitaph in the prison paper there a year later, when he hung himself with his belt.

The Eglin Federal Prison Camp was composed of a big wooden administration building, four big old rickety World War II surplus Air Force barracks, a wooden chow hall, and a few other miscellaneous frame buildings for the clinic, library, and education department. All arranged in a little circle, and surrounded all the way around by a little red clay road — tying in the whole ten acres or so.

And the red clay road was our only fence. Our only bars.

"Let me tell you right off the bat," the warden said to us the next morning at our orientation class, "you're not here to get rehabilitated! You're here to provide cheap labor for the United States Air Force. And as long as you work hard and do your job and obey the rules, you can stay here in this exclusive little country club. But foul up for one second — and you're going to Atlanta. Or Leavenworth."

"And if you want to escape," he continued, "just be my guest! Just go ahead and walk off. We won't even chase you. We'll just call the FBI and let them come after you. And I can tell you — they always catch you. They never miss!"

And he was just about right.

A broken old alcoholic, our warden was 'in the bag' just about all day long. Every day. But prison will do that to you. Whether you're an inmate or whether you're a guard. Eventually, it'll tear you down.

234

"4-D-21's your bunk number, Neill," Old John laughed. "The best bunk in the whole joint. Now go on down to the clothing exchange and draw your uniforms. The next count's at five. And don't miss the count! Cause they take that awfully seriously around here!"

They took it seriously everywhere in the Federal system.

"The count" is the way they make sure everybody is where he's supposed to be. They count every prisoner in the Federal system about every two hours and report the count in to Washington by teletype. And at nighttime you'd better leave an arm, or a leg or something sticking out from under the blanket where they can see that it's a real body. And not just some stuffing. Because otherwise they'll come tear the blanket off you to make sure you're there. And if anyone is missing at a count, you have to stay right in your cell or by your bunk until he's found.

I remember one guy was missing from one count at Springfield. But all they found of him were his feet. And they were still in his shoes. The rest of his clothes were folded and stacked neatly nearby. But it was in the kitchen. Right by the huge industrial meat grinder. Some of the convicts apparently had run him on through.

But life was exciting there for me at Eglin. All I did was just praise the Lord and read the Bible all day long. And do a little typing for the Administration once in a while.

I started out as a clerk typist in the parole records office under Mr. Henry. He was a nice man who tried to help the convicts all he could. And when the best job in the prison camp came up for grabs, he helped me get it.

235

"Safety clerk."

The senior lieutenant, James A. Foster, was the "Safety Officer" for the camp. It was sort of a make-believe red tape job the Air Force made the prison go through. And Foster needed somebody to do his typing for him. And what a neat job it was!

I had my own private little air-conditioned office with an electric typewriter. And all the books and Bibles I wanted. And I could just stay in the office all day long — or even at night if I wanted to — and read and pray and write.

I even had my own key to the office, and I could lock myself in. If a guard wanted in, he had to knock on the door and ask me to let him in. And that used to burn some of them up a little bit. But God always has an incredible way of taking care of His own! And He really took care of me. Because He knew I wanted to study and learn His Word - backwards and forwards.

And that's what I did. Because I could do all of the Safety Clerk typing in an hour or two each week. And the rest of the time I just studied the Bible and prayed.

And then in a few weeks, there was Dorothy and the kids! She had sold the house in Miami and moved up to Fort Walton Beach — lock, stock and barrel. Even brought my mother along for good measure. They rented a house in Fort Walton Beach. And we started settling down to prison life.

Dorothy got a job as a legal secretary and put the kids in school. And I guess she'd only been there a couple of months when the same thing happened to her that happened to me on that little cell floor.

She had seen the incredible love and joy and peace that just overflowed in my life now. She had seen a new power in me. And a new strength and vitality. And when I told her about the wonderful secret things God was doing in my life there in the prison camp—she wanted the same thing to happen to her.

She wanted the same kind of love and joy and peace and triumph and victory that she saw in my life.

And so she asked for it. With all her heart.

All alone in her car, parked in the lot of an A & W Root Beer drive-in restaurant, for the first time in her life she truly asked the Lord Jesus Christ to take over her life. She gave her whole life to Him there that day. And she became born of the Spirit of God.

A few weeks later we both matriculated as students at the Liberty Bible College in Pensacola. I began working on a Master's Degree in Theology, and Dorothy was taking the same courses — except on an undergraduate level.

She would drive forty-five miles every morning to the school and tape the lectures. And then drive forty-five miles home. And on Saturdays she would bring a tape player into the visiting yard there at the prison camp, and I would listen to seven hours of Bible lectures. Then I would go back into my barracks and try to get it all down on paper so that I could remember it all. Then the next day she would come back and I would listen to seven more hours of lectures. Sitting out there on the concrete benches in the visiting yard.

The Holy Spirit is a wonderful teacher! And at the end of the first quarter, we both had an "A" average.

But about that time, Lieutenant Foster began feeling a little sorry for me, and he came into the office with a surprise for me one day.

"Neill, this is my tape recorder here," he indicated as he walked into the office with one of my wife's two tape players in his hand, "and I'm going to keep it here in my office. And I don't want anybody to touch it. And I don't want it to leave this office! But if by any chance you should have any use for it, well, you go ahead and help yourself."

And he turned and shot out of the office leaving me with my mouth hanging open before I could even gather my wits enough to thank him.

He was sneaking it in to me! Against the rules.

Not long after, he made arrangements for the prison's Education Department to allow the tapes to be mailed to them by the Bible College. And they gave them to me there in the prison camp so I could study without having to give up my visiting time.

By now I had every one of the major translations of the Bible, and a map of the Holy Lands up on the wall. I really made a seminary out of that little Safety Office!

238

I would lay all of the Bibles out on the table there in the office and start reading them simultaneously, side by side, from cover to cover. Beginning with Genesis 1:1 in each of the translations. And then Genesis 1:2 in each of the translations. And I'd go ali the way through. And when I came to a discrepancy of some sort, I'd stop and look up the Greek or Hebrew or Aramaic in the lexicons. I'd resolve the discrepancy if it could be resolved, and those few which I couldn't, I simply made a note of the differences.

1 read them backwards and forwards. Over and over and over.

I must have read the Bible from cover to cover close to fifty times before I was released from the penitentiary. And though I read some of the paraphrases, I didn't much care for them. I thought God wrote His Word just the way He wanted it.

In my spare time, I even read some of the cult books. I wanted to know what they said because you can combat an enemy better if you know him.

We didn't have a chaplain there at first, but the other Christian convicts and I were held our own little prayer meetings and Bible studies. What few of us Christians there were, had a wonderful time praising the Lord and fellowshipping and lifting up the name of Jesus around the prison camp.

And then along came our new chaplain - Chaplain Stump! Wow!

Didn't even own a Bible! Didn't believe that any man should give his heart to the Lord Jesus while he was in prison!

"There are too many unusual pressures and circumstances in here." He used to say. "So if you want to get saved, wait til you get out in the free world to do it. Don't do it in here!"

He even tried to keep us from getting Bibles. *He made it against the rules for us to worship or fellowship together anymore.* In fact, he made it an absolute rule that no two Christians were ever allowed to meet together for Bible study or for prayer or for worship.

I went to the warden about it. But he backed up the chaplain.

"Listen, Neill! I'm a Christian, too." The warden rather boldly exaggerated. "And if I want to worship God, I can just come into my office here and do it all by myself! So if you want to worship God, you just do it all by yourself, too!"

But of course — just like the persecution of the early Christians in Rome — this only made us stronger. Now the handful of us Christians who were there really met in earnest. Clandestinely. But we worshipped God with a new fervor and with a new intensity.

God always triumphs! And so do His people. And all of us Christian convicts just showered more and more love on old Chaplain Stump every time we'd see him.

And the months rolled on by. It was the greatest time of my life! Dorothy and I were almost completely broke by now. But oh, our immeasurable riches in Glory!

Each new dawn I was out on the compound under the big old oak trees festooned with Spanish moss — lifting my head to the heavens and just praising God and praying in the Spirit and thanking Him and fellowshipping with Him.

And many times at night I'd sit out under the trees with the moon shining through — praising God and thanking Him for making me His. Thanking Him for giving me that one last chance. For giving me this incredible new life. And our loving Father just showered the gifts and fruit of His Holy Spirit upon me in His inimitable abundance. His matchless love! *And I couldn't have been happier if I had been a billionaire! And on the streets!*

I had learned what it really truly means to rejoice in the Lord always!

I had found an old beat up copy of Merlin Carothers' book Power in Praise. And I must have read it three or four times. It really opened up new vistas in dynamic and victorious Christian living to me. In fact it so impressed me that I had Dorothy buy dozens of copies of it. And I would sneak them past our kindly black Methodist preacher / prison guard in the visiting room and distribute them to the men in the camp.

I even praised the Lord for the cockroaches! And they just seemed to disappear. *I rejoiced for all the mosquitoes!* And they disappeared too. I just began living completely and totally and constantly in praise and thanksgiving and rejoicing. Praying always without ceasing.

And my fifty year sentence disappeared too!

"Neill, get your gear together! You're goin' home!" Lieutenant Foster yelled at me one day!

"Dear God, did I hear him right? Did he say 'You're going home?!'"

I'd been there only two years. And I had never asked God to let me out. And I had never asked man to let me out.

But now God was opening the gates for me! Free at last! Thank God Almighty, I was free at last!

I sprinted two hundred yards up the compound to my caseworker's office in the Administration Building. And I guess he must have seen me coming, because he had it in his hand when I got there!

"Neill, they've made a mistake! They've made a big mistake in Washington! But there's nothing I can do about it." He teased me. "You're goin' home. Here's your parole!"

My parole.

A little slip of paper with my name and number on the top and a date in the middle and somebody's signature on the bottom. That's all there was to it.

And the date in the middle of the page was the day after Thanksgiving that year, 1973. *The day after Thanksgiving!* God was going to make me spend Thanksgiving Day there giving thanks to Him.

And boy did I ever!

242

I guess I gave thanks to God that last day in prison like nobody in the whole world has ever thanked Him. I sang to Him, and I whistled to Him, and I cried to Him, and I prayed to Him! I even did something very few human beings have ever done. I got out my tattered old Bible and I opened it up to my favorite scriptures. And one by one, I read them to Almighty God.

"Listen to this one, Father...!"

The Lord is my Shepherd; I shall not want.

He maketh me to lie down in green pastures;

He leadeth me beside the still waters.

He restoreth my soul.

He leadeth me in paths of righteousness for His name's sake."

"Isn't that beautiful, Father! That's just so beautiful! I love it so much!"

That Thanksgiving Day, in November of 1973, I had been in the penitentiary exactly two years and thirteen days.

And I ought to still be there! Considering the things I did and the life I lived — I ought to still be there. And there's just no way in the natural I could have gotten out in that short a period of time. They never let anybody go home that soon if they've done the kind of things I did.

243

There are thousands of men in prison today who have been there for twenty-five or thirty or even forty years who have done a lot less than what I did.

But then they've never found Jesus. Or His Amazing Grace.

Oh, that amazing grace, how sweet the sound, that saved a wretch like me. I once indeed was lost! Oh, but now I'm found! I was blind, but now I see!

And like a child on Christmas Day, our heavenly Father had a great big whopping present waiting for me under the tree when I woke up the next morning.

My first day in the free world!

14   "LO, I AM WITH YOU ALWAYS!"

It was just turning first light. And it must have been about forty-five degrees that crisp windy November dawn.

"O.K.! Get lost, convict!" The friendly hack smiled. "You can go home now!"

And I walked out the front door of that prison camp a free man. And Oh, I mean really free!

And there — out in the parking lot — waiting for me in the morning cold, were my wife and children and more than two dozen lovely spirit-filled Christians!

Baptists and Methodists and Pentecostals and Catholics. And they all hugged and kissed me and cried. And hugged each other and cried.

Even Lt. Foster and Bill Barron, the convict ex-governor of West Virginia, came out and cried.

"Come on, everybody! Let's all get out of here and go buy this convict some breakfast!" Bo Britt laughed as he threw his arm around me and led me over to one of the cars.

And like the children of Abraham, we all went filing down the road in a big Christian caravan to a nearby restaurant. And did it ever feel funny. Me - riding in a car down a street! Just like I hadn't been in prison at all.

And of course I had never been baptized. So you can guess where all those Christians took me that cold morning right after breakfast.

Right!

Straight over to the Gulf of Mexico, about five miles away from the prison camp. And the sun was just barely peeking over the horizon as Jim Cotton and I sloshed out into the frigid surf.

Jim had been a lawyer at one time, involved in politics in the State capitol in Tallahassee. But then he got disbarred and met the Lord that way. And he really loved the Lord. And I loved Jim. And that's why I asked him to baptize me.

But the Gulf of Mexico there at Fort Walton Beach shoals off very gradually. So we had to walk about fifty yards or so off-shore before we could get into water deep enough to bury me. And by the time we got out that far — with the icy waves splashing over us — poor skinny Jim was shaking so badly he could hardly talk.

But then he put one hand on my chest and one on my back and got all ready to baptize me.

"Gene, how do you want me to baptize you?" His teeth chattered through blue lips.

"What do you mean *how*? How many ways are there?" I grinned back at him.

"Well, you know," he shook, "some people baptize just in the name of Jesus. But others baptize in the name of the Father and of the Son and of the Holy Ghost!"

"Gee, I don't know, Jim! God loves you and He loves me. So whatever seems the proper way to you suits me."

"Well, all right then, Gene Neill," he did his best to assume a very serious and ecclesiastical air as he shook from the cold, "is Jesus Christ really the Lord of your life?"

"Jim, you know He is!" I smiled seriously.

"Well, in that event," he boomed in his best pulpit baritone, "I baptize you in the name of the Father — and of the Son — and of the Holy Ghost!"

But then he paused.

He paused a long time. I guess he just wasn't sure he had it right yet. But then his eyes lit up. And he smiled as another thought flashed into his mind. . . .

"But most of all — I baptize you in the precious and the wonderful name of our Lord Jesus Christ!"

247

And down he shoved me into the freezing cold water.

"PRAISE THE LORD!" I laughed as I came back up out of the surf. And Jim and I hugged and cried as the icy waves broke all around us.

Back up on the beach and in some dry clothes, we all shared the body and blood of our Lord Jesus there in a little circle. Gathered around in a huddle with the wind whistling through. Bread and grape juice.

And nobody felt the icy wind. Only the Spirit of Jesus. And love. And everybody cried some more. And hugged each other some more. And praised God and gave thanks to Him for setting a poor wretch like me free *on the day after Thanksgiving!*

Then we drove the fifty miles west to Pensacola to a little community called Beulah. "Beulah land." I like to call it. Where Dorothy was living in a house trailer down a little dirt road out in the woods. And there we spent the rest of the day in thanksgiving and praise and worship to our Lord. Singing songs and reading the Bible and lifting up the Lord Jesus.

And that night my family and I gathered around our little wooden table there in the house trailer and ate supper together. For the first time in two years and thirteen days.

And it sure felt funny!

It even felt funny not having guards coming through counting me every two hours! It wasn't so much that I had been gone for the two

248

years and thirteen days. But it was the thought that I might have been gone forever.

And the queen-sized bed felt strange after all those nights in smoke-filled little prison cells on hard prison cots.

For the next few months I did odd jobs around Pensacola — painting houses and installing air conditioners and the like.

We didn't have a dime. We didn't even own a car. My only clothes were a couple of pairs of bib overalls and a shirt or two.

But I had Jesus!

And I had learned in my years in prison that He was all I need. I learned that as long as He is with me, I didn't want for anything. Or need anything. Or lack anything. He is all sufficient.

He is my Shepherd! And He always will be.

I remember a Christian medical doctor from Thomasville, Georgia who visited me one time while I was in prison. And I told him how God was just right there with me and how He talked with me, and how He comforted me. How He was just so very close to me every second. But my friend really frightened me for the first time since I had met the Lord.

"Gene, I don't want to disillusion you in your new walk with God," he spoke the authority of his many years as a Christian, *"but God is not always going to be there with you.* There are going to be times when He withdraws from you and you won't feel His presence. Or hear

249

Him. Or know where He is. And you'll just have to proceed on raw faith. *Without Him."*

And I was terrified. For God was all I had.

I couldn't wait until he left the visiting room so I could go back and talk with my heavenly Father again. And I ran back into the dark little chapel and threw myself down on my knees.

"God! Oh God! Are you going to leave me like he said! Father, are you going to leave me!"

"I will never leave you, Gene." He answered. "I will be with you until the end of time."

And indeed He was. And is.

But then one day God spoke to me and said, "Gene, I want you to go to California now. I have a work for you there which I want you to accomplish." And He confirmed it to Dorothy. And the day He told us we had a total of *three cents.*

Only three pennies in the whole world. And we still didn't have a car or clothing or much of anything. But *Oh*, He does provide!

He gave us a rickety old 1960 GMC V-6 gasoline powered 66 passenger school bus to drive to California. And it was really something else! It had been junked by the Okaloosa County School System, and then purchased by a waterfront rescue mission. And now they were selling it.

It was double junk! And it wouldn't run. The engine was frozen up and the transmission wouldn't work. And there was no battery in it. But it was what the Lord had provided. And that's always more than enough.

So we towed it out to our trailer that night, and the next morning I started working on it. I pulled the intake manifold and the exhaust manifold and the heads and started working on the frozen piston. But then I realized the transmission was frozen up too. So we towed it into a transmission garage, and they started in on it too.

And Dorothy's brother, Alan Bullock, was living with us now. He had been miraculously delivered from drugs by the Lord about a month or so after I was released from prison, and he had moved up with us that week.

So while the mechanics were working on the engine and transmission, Alan and I were pulling the seats out and building bunks and partitions and making a camper out of it. All without any money.

And the transmission man said we'd never find any parts for the transmission. Not even in a junkyard.

But God had told me we were going to leave Pensacola on the 21st day of that month. So I knew we were.

But when the 21st rolled around, the engine was still torn apart. The transmission was lying out on the ground in pieces. And we didn't even have enough money to fill the gas tank with gasoline.

But we gathered around the bus that day and took our problem to our heavenly Father. We asked Him to please help us with the problem. And to please somehow get us out of there that day.

We had hardly opened our eyes after praying when a man drove up in a pickup truck with a 1958 Cadillac hydromatic transmission which he had found in a junkyard. And when they pulled it all apart moments later, they discovered that it had just *exactly the parts we needed.*

And about two hours later the Lord miraculously provided the money we needed to pay the garage bill, fill the gas tank and get out of town.

And before dark we were on our way. Just as He had promised. Dorothy and the kids and Alan and I and our German Shepherd dog. And pots and pans and army blankets. And a Styrofoam ice box and groceries and clothes. And about fifteen Bibles. In that rickety old school bus.

Heading for California! Like the "Grapes of Wrath!"

And the story of how we got there without any money in that old school bus would fill a whole book! But God just simply provided as we went along. For all our needs.

But now let me tell you a little something about theology: Christians all over the world are just incessantly arguing about a thing they call "eternal security." That is, some folks say you can backslide and some folks say you can't. And the whole thing isn't worth arguing about. But this one thing I know: our old school bus was eternally secure!

We drove that old fire-spittin', back-firing, smoking, rattling piece of junk all the way from Pensacola, Florida, clear across America to Huntington Beach, California, *with no reverse gear.*

You couldn't backslide! You had to keep going forward!

One way with Jesus!

But we hadn't had a chance to paint our "Chariot of Israel" before we left Pensacola, so we stopped en route and gave her a first class homemade paint job. We rented a little ten dollar spray gun which didn't work too well, masked her up and put on a thick coat of bright canary yellow paint!

Then on one side of the bus — in great big four foot red and blue letters — I painted *"Jesus is Lord!"* On the other side of the bus — again in great big four foot blue and red letters — I painted *"Jesus is the Way!"* And on the back *"Praise the Lord!"* And on the front, *"The King is Coming."*

We didn't know a whole lot about theology. Or even much about Christianity. But when we drove down the road, everybody knew whose side we were on! We took real seriously the scriptural admonition that the redeemed of the Lord should say so!

And although I don't guess we looked particularly poor, people would come visit us while we were camping, or even stop us on the highway, and give us clothes or groceries or money. God just did

253

more abundantly than we could ask or think. And He just always — always — supplied our every need according to His riches in glory in Christ Jesus!

We short-change God so often! We just don't really let Him take over and show His might on our behalf. We don't give Him a chance to work miracles for us. We always want to do it ourselves. I guess because we don't trust Him.

But it's easy to turn it all over to Him when you don't have any choice. It was easy for us to believe in miracles. Because if we were going to eat we had to. Just like me down in that little solitary cell — it was easy to give up my whole life — every fiber of my life for the Lord Jesus Christ — because I didn't have anything left. I was a dead man.

But God will let you have anything that your eyes of faith can see. Absolutely anything! The Bible says in seven different places that you can ask God for whatever you will — and you shall receive it!

And since we didn't know any better than to believe — we received! Like the time in May when we got to a place called Flagstaff, Arizona!

Our little ones, Heather and Gene, were nine and six at the time. And of course since they were from sunny southern Florida, they had never seen snow. But I had always told them, since they started visiting me when I was in prison, that the Bible means exactly what it says! And that those seven places where it says you can ask God for anything you want — and He'll give it to you — mean just exactly that.

So that sunshiny and cloudless day as were rolling down the highway there by Flagstaff, little nine year old Heather came up and put her arm around me. The windows of the bus were open and I was driving in a short-sleeved shirt and was very comfortable.

When she laid the bombshell on me.

"Daddy, would it be silly for us to ask God to make it snow today?" She asked me, as seriously as her little heart knew how. And if I had been anything but a firm believer in a real miracle-working God, I'd have thought of some way of talking her out of that snow right then and there! I could have said it was silly. Or that it might cause too many accidents on the highway because people were unprepared for snow. Or my old con-man mind could have thought of a dozen other reasons why she shouldn't want it to snow that day.

But I just happen to serve a miracle-working Master.

"Honey," I smiled at her, "if it's important to you — I'm sure it would be important to God."

"Oh boy!" Heather exclaimed, as she dashed back into the rear of the bus dragging little Gene with her.

"Come on, Gene! Let's go pray!"

And I watched them in the rearview mirror as they knelt back there. With the palms of their little hands pressed together and held up to their chins — in the old-fashioned prayer way. And they prayed for a long time. I could see their mouths moving as they prayed. But finally they ran back up to the front of the bus. And Heather put her

255

arm around me again and just stood there looking out the windshield. Waiting for it to snow.

Knowing that it would. Because He had promised.

Yet there still wasn't a cloud in the sky. And it wasn't a bit colder. And if I had been a gambling man, there are no kind of odds I wouldn't have taken on the probabilities of a flurry that afternoon.

But our King breaks all kinds of odds.

And He had promised them snow.

And as God is my witness, in fifteen minutes I had to pull our old rickety school bus off the road and park. *Because there was so much snow on the windshield I couldn't see out it anymore.*

The windshield wipers were vacuum operated ones, and they just quit working altogether. But they had little handles on the inside of the bus. Something like a jeep does. And I grabbed those handles and tried to keep the snow off by swishing the blades back and forth across the windshield. But I couldn't get it off.

So we all piled out of the bus and started throwing snow balls. Everyone — including the dog — played until they were tired and hoarse.

It was almost supper time. And we managed to drive on to the next 7-11 where we bought groceries for supper.

But there was the proprietor. Standing out on the curb. Just looking up at the sky. Watching those big silvery flakes of snow — just floating down so peacefully.

"Don't understand it!" He half muttered to me as he gazed up at the sky. "This sure isn't what the weatherman predicted! Isn't it crazy, snow on a day like this!"

And I started to tell him the whole story. But then I figured, *"Oh well, what's the use!"*

But we pushed on to California, where life really got interesting!

First of all, we didn't have a place to sleep when we got here. We didn't have any money to rent or buy a place in which to sleep. So — we just lived in the bus! Simple as that.

For five months.

And we slept in parking lots. And along streets. In gas stations and in County parks. And along the highways. All kinds of places!

And we immediately began attending classes in the evenings at the Melodyland School of Theology, while I started looking for a job. And that was a real gas!

I suppose it was just God's way of dealing with a whole lot of folks through me. But He sure did bounce me around a lot job hunting.

Like the time I answered the ad for a job as a gas station attendant near Melodyland.

257

"I'm here in response to your ad in the paper for a gas station attendant." I smiled pleasantly at the proprietor. "I've had some experience. I'm a good mechanic and I've done a lot of grease work. And I'm willing to work hard."

"O.K. Just sit down over there and fill in this application blank." He told me.

"Application blank." I thought to myself. *"Oh, wow!* Who would have thought they would have an application blank for a job like this! Oh well, here goes...."

And everything went along smoothly until I got to the part about education. But they only had two lines. One line for grammar school and one line for high school. But I have ten years of college. Five years of undergraduate study and five years on a graduate level. And I've been to six different colleges and universities — all over the world.

"Well, I'm a Christian." I thought to myself. "So I've got to tell the truth." And so I wrote it in. In real fine print. And out in the margin and sideways and all around. Until I finally got it in.

Then I flipped the form over; and everything went along pretty smoothly until the last two questions. And they were real bummers!

"Have you ever been arrested for a crime?"

"If so, what was the disposition?"

"Well, praise the Lord! Here I go again...." I thought to myself. And on the first line I wrote, "Yes." And on the second line I wrote, "Sentenced to 50 years."

Then I handed the paper to the man and stood back and watched.

And I wish you could have seen his face.

He didn't know whether to curse me or run from me. Or laugh at me. And even after he read it completely, he turned it back over to the front side and just sort of stared at it dumbly trying to think of something to say to me.

"Yeah! Well. . . ok . . . eh . . . I'll give you a ring if we need you."

And that was the end of that interview.

But the same kind of thing happened at a company down in Santa Ana, California, called "Allergan." It's a great big building which covers about a whole city block. And about five stories tall. And apparently they make some kind of pharmaceuticals. But they had an ad in the paper for an "animal tender." In their experimental laboratory, they have little rats and mice in cages. And they wanted somebody to keep the cages clean and to feed the rats and the mice.

And God sent me all the way down there to apply for that job!

But there came the old application form!

I put down the same ten years of college and the same six universities in the education section. And the same fifty years for the disposition question. And when I handed it to the personnel director, I got the same kind of soft-shoe shuffle I had gotten from the gas station attendant.

"Well ... ah ... yes ... Dr. Neill . . . ah . . . glad to have met you . . . and ... ah ... we will surely call you . . . ah ... or ... ah . . . we'll drop you a line as soon as we make a decision on this matter."

I couldn't even get a job feeding rats!

But I got the greatest job in the whole world. Or at least my kids thought so.

I was driving down the street in Santa Ana, California, when I saw a big building there with a large sign *permanently* painted on the side of the stucco — *"HELP WANTED."* And I knew if they had to paint it on the side of their building in six-foot letters — that meant that they were really hurting for somebody all year around.

And they were...

It was the Tropical Ice Cream Company. And they have a whole fleet of trucks with little loud-speaker type bells up on the front of the trucks. And big windows cut In the side. And they drive around the neighborhood selling popsicles and fudge bars and ice cream sandwiches and long johns.

And you should see old "Perry Mason" hustlin' those Long John ice cream bars!

Because that's exactly what I did the summer of 1974.

And I plastered Jesus stickers all over the truck. On the front and on the sides and on the back. And even inside where the kids stick their heads in to pick out their ice cream or candy. One great big poster right on the ice cream freezer looked like an airline travel poster. And loudly proclaimed, *"FLY THE FRIENDLY SKIES OF JESUS!"*

And business was pretty good.

But then I met Amy. Amy De Jong — the little saint who ran the bookstore at the Melodyland Christian Center. And I was making $125 a week. Until Amy prayed for me that day.

I had gone into the bookstore to buy the stickers for my ice cream truck when I met Amy. But I ended up telling her the story of my life and what I was going to use her poster for, and she grabbed me and pulled me back into the office where her husband was.

"Let's pray for this man's ice cream business!" She said.

And boy did she pray!

"Oh, dear Father," she earnestly pleaded, "just bring so many people up to this man's truck to buy ice cream that he won't even have enough ice cream to sell to them! Oh Father, just make him run out of ice cream! Just let him sell every piece of ice cream and candy that he has. Every day! Just bless him Lord. Oh, just bless him in a wonderful way!"

And I still have the written receipts to prove that the very next day my sales began to increase until they were almost double what they had been before Amy prayed.

And we continued there at the Melodyland School of Theology — still living in the bus through the first two quarters — until September 1974.

Then God told me it was time for me to start ministering *full time,* though I had been ministering here and there since I got out of prison.

In fact the first Sunday out of prison I preached my first sermon at the New Hope Afro-Methodist Episcopal Church in Pensacola, Florida - the sweet little black church pastored by the same prison guard who used to let me sneak in Bibles and crosses to the other men there in the prison camp.

And I had been preaching and sharing my testimony ever since. But I guess God thought I was ready to do a little bit more.

So I quit my popsicle selling job and started preaching and teaching and sharing my testimony full time.

And I have been in a full time evangelistic and prison ministry ever since.

I was eventually ordained as a Southern Baptist minister by the Forest Drive Baptist Church of Columbia, South Carolina.

And I've been in more prisons and talked with more convicts than anyone else I know of.

This book is in its seventeenth printing in English and has also been published in Korean, Swedish, Greek and Spanish.

And what a thrilling life!

Like the first trip I made back to Miami shortly after I got out of prison. It was the first time I had been there since I left in chains. A convict.

I walked right back up into those criminal courtrooms with my Bible in my hand. And I went to visit all the old judges. And the cops and robbers and junkies and dopies and prostitutes whom I used to know. And I told them all about a real and living Jesus whom I had met in a little solitary cell. I told them how He had transformed my life. And how he had given me a new start. A wonderful new start. *Just filled with love and happiness and peace!*

And I told them about how He loves them. And about how I love them.

And one of them was Ray Havens. The same Detective Ray Havens, of the Organized Crime Division, who pointed his pistol at my head that night and put me up against the wall. And I hadn't seen him since then.

"God bless you, Ray! I'm glad to see you!" I smiled. "And I just want to tell you that I thank you for sending me to prison. Because it was the greatest thing that ever happened to me! The greatest thing in my whole life. But let's go across the street to your office because I want to tell you about a man named Jesus whom I met in a little cell out there in Missouri

And I laid it on him. For about an hour and a half. I told him about how Jesus had transformed my life. I didn't get him down on his knees to pray. But I'll bet that night, when he hit the sack, he thrashed around a long time before he got any sleep.

And I sought out my old private investigator. The one who had gone to the police and ratted on me. And I told him about my Jesus. And that I loved him. And that Jesus loves him. And he'll not soon forget it either.

I tried to tell Jim Stanfill, the man who had really "sold me down the river." My old pal who brought the Federal agent in to buy my cocaine from me. And of all the people on the whole face of planet earth — I wanted to tell him about Jesus. But I was too late.

"Where can I find Jim Stanfill?" I asked Ray Havens as I talked with him there in the Organized Crime Division.

"You're not going to find him." Ray answered. "He was killed. You'll never tell him about Jesus."

And then there was Jack Lloyd.

If there was any one man who was really responsible for putting the case against me together— it was a man named Jack Lloyd.

At the time of my arrest, Jack was in charge of the Federal Bureau of Narcotics and Dangerous Drugs in Miami, Florida. A big time "narc." And he was all cop. A cop's cop. He really wanted to see me go away. And I don't blame him.

I hadn't seen Jack since I went to the Penitentiary. 'Till I talked to him that day on the phone. Long distance to his new assignment in Dallas.

"Jack, I'm going to be coming through Dallas on my way back to California. And I'm going to be preaching in the Episcopal Church of the Resurrection there. And I would just give a million dollars if you'd come by and hear me." I urged him cordially.

"Gene, I wouldn't miss it for a million dollars!" He shot back.

I don't think he really believed me. I think he thought I was running some kind of con game. And he was going to come by and see what my racket was.

But Father Ted Nelson, the Rector of that incredibly lovely church, had asked me to share my testimony with the brethren there that Friday night. And so I did. For about an hour and a half. I told them what a rotten bum I'd been all my life. How I'd been an atheist and finally wound up in prison. And how I'd called out to a God I didn't believe in from the floor of that little solitary cell. I told them the whole story.

And then I told them about Jack Lloyd.

"The man who really put me in the penitentiary — the one man who really got me my time — is right here in this room tonight!" I told them. "Jack I can't see you back out there for these lights in my eyes. Where are you, Jack?"

And then I saw his hand go up. Back on the side of the church by the wall.

And of course all those crazy Christians started giving him a tremendous ovation! *Applauding him* — for having sent me to prison! Well, praise the Lord! I did too.

But as the service drew to a close, Father Ted and a couple of other priests came forward to administer the Eucharist. The Lord's Supper. And Father Ted almost made an altar call out of his invitation to the Eucharist.

"This is really the body and blood of our Lord Jesus Christ which we're going to share together this evening." He instructed them solemnly. "And we would invite *any* of you to come down here and share these sacraments with us — if Jesus Christ is truly the Lord of your life. Or if you would like for Jesus to come into your life and to be your Lord — then we would welcome you, too. Come down front here, and join us in this Holy Sacrament."

And he and the other priests and I began serving the unleavened bread and the wine together. On my side of that altar, Father Ted was serving the little wafers of unleavened bread. And I had the chalice with the wine and was giving each of the people who came forward a little sip.

266

Almost the entire congregation had come to the altar and left, when suddenly I saw him.

There on his knees at God's Holy Altar, to share the body and blood of our resurrected and risen and living Lord Jesus Christ — *was Jack Lloyd. That cop!*

Here we were! The cop and the robber! Sharing the holiest of all sacraments. The body and blood of the Savior of the world.

Oh Hallelujah! I could just hear the angels sing as they saw the two of us together there. In love and worship of our Lord Jesus Christ.

Our heavenly Father is so full of miracles and surprises and gifts.

He's healed all the old wounds. My former wife and our two children, and Dorothy and I and our children, all went to church together some years ago in Atlanta. And we praised God together— sitting in the same pew. A wound that only a miracle-working God could heal.

And He's given me opportunities to carry His glorious Gospel message to many millions of people all over the world! To tell them about His love.

I've ministered all over America, Mexico, Central America, Puerto Rico, England, Sweden, Spain, Bangladesh, France, Canada, Norway, Germany, Greece, Italy, South Korea, Uganda, Kenya, Israel and *the old Soviet Union. Some 40 countries in all, give or take.*

In fact I was arrested three times during my three-month ministry in the Soviet Union.

Once in a tiny Gregorian monastery down near the Turkish border, when they came after me with two truckloads of Russian soldiers with *submachine guns and attack dogs!*

And a second time when the KGB (Soviet Secret Police) kicked in the door of a tiny apartment in the village of Ararat where I had gone to minister to a group of the "under-ground" Christians.

And a third time I was arrested in the city of Kishinev, where the police slammed me up against the wall and tore my shirt and overcoat.

But, you see, there's a real risen Lord Jesus Christ who has a kingdom all His own. Where we can go and take all our problems and cast them on Him. And He'll take them. For He cares for us. A real-risen Lord Jesus who is the same yesterday, today and forever! And who will never leave us. Not even until the end of time.

Oh, beloved, He is! And was! And always shall be! The beginning and the end. King of Kings and Lord of Lords for me!

My Master and my friend!

EPILOGUE

This book has no ending. Only a beginning. Because in God's Kingdom that's the way it is.

And life for me and my family has become — ever since that infinite moment on the filthy floor of that tiny solitary cell — an adventure to end all adventures. A thrilling and vibrant and laughter-filled calliope excursion through a lifetime of love and joy and peace in the Holy Spirit.

I've lived an unbelievable life.

I've journeyed to the ends of the earth. Lived for years in cities of the Orient and in Europe where most travel only in their fondest flights of fantasy. With ten years in six different universities and colleges, I have sought after knowledge and truth as very few have done. As a public defender and prosecutor and successful criminal defense attorney, I did what millions only dream of doing as they watch television and the great silver screen. I've owned everything you can buy on earth. I've been a leader in the underworld. And with a fifty-year prison sentence in solitary confinement, I've journeyed to the very deepest bowels of the valley of the shadow of death.

Yet through it all I have come to know for an absolute certainty that there is only one truth in life. Only one ingredient. Only one thing that really matters.

The King of Kings. And Lord of Lords. The Lamb of God.

Jesus.

All else is folly.

Meaningless.

And thus for me — for the rest of my life — as one of my dearest Christian brothers so poignantly put it one day long past:

"... forgetting those things which are behind, and reaching forth unto those things which are before, I press toward the mark for the prize of the high calling of God in Christ Jesus."

-Gene Neill

Comments and inquiries should be directed to:

The Voice of Triumph, Inc.

P. O. Box 78

Mayo, Florida 32066

Email: gneillministries@gmail.com

Website: geneneill.com or go-to-jail.org

See your local Christian bookstore or contact

The Voice of Triumph, Inc. directly for copies

of *I'm Gonna Bury You!* (Also available in the

Spanish language.)